When *Love* Filled *the* Gap

D1595967

LaJoyce Martin

When Love Filled the Gap

When Love Filled The Gap

by LaJoyce Martin

©1988 Word Aflame Press
  Hazelwood, MO 63042-2299

Cover Design by Tim Agnew

Cover Art by Art Kirchoff

All Scripture quotations in this book are from the King James Version of the Bible unless otherwise identified.

Printed in United States of America.

Printed by

Library of Congress Cataloging-in-Publication Data

Martin, LaJoyce, 1937–
    When love filled the gap.

    I. Title.
PS3563.A72486W44   1988   813'.54   87-37241
ISBN 0-932581-30-7

To
my Dearest Friend,
without whose Spirit I cannot live

Contents

Chapter 1 – Memory's Eddy *11*

Chapter 2 – The Argument *19*

Chapter 3 – The Returned Wheel *27*

Chapter 4 – Martha's Proposal *33*

Chapter 5 – The Strange Dream *39*

Chapter 6 – A New Idea *47*

Chapter 7 – Arthur's Arrival *53*

Chapter 8 – Dinner with the Mayor *59*

Chapter 9 – A Fishing Trip *65*

Chapter 10 – The Superintendent's Visit *71*

Chapter 11 – Overheard Plans *77*

Chapter 12 – Unwanted Visitor *83*

Chapter 13 – Bridge Washout! *91*

Chapter 14 – A Seeking Student *97*

Chapter 15 – A Miserable Night *103*

Chapter 16 – Miracles.......................... *109*

Chapter 17 – A Changed Man *115*

Chapter 18 – The Watchman's Inquisition *121*

Chapter 19 – Illness *127*

Chapter 20 – A Conflicting Story *133*

Chapter 21 – Dismissed *139*

Chapter 22 – House Hunting..................... *145*

Chapter 23 – Heart Battle *151*

Chapter 24 – The Council Meeting *157*

Chapter 25 – Straightening out the Facts *163*

Chapter 26 – Home for Thanksgiving *169*
Chapter 27 – A Futile Visit *175*
Chapter 28 – Nathan's Resignation *181*
Chapter 29 – God's Mysterious Ways *187*
Chapter 30 – Dessie's Rainbow *193*

Acknowledgements

In the darkest days of my life, God sent some special "rainbows" with words of love and encouragement. Among those to whom such acknowledgments are due are Carole Terry, Madalene Waldrep, Dolores Neely, Glenda McGuire, Sandra Myer, Glendell Pate, Grace Jinks, Nona Freeman, Jan Daniels, Lorene Berry (my mother), Cynthia Rennels, Fay Martin (my mother-in-law), Shirley Tatum, Mary Wallace, Teresa Manning, Judy Whitley, Eileen Fairchild, Jacklin McFall, Ruth Cremeans, Mary Ruth Broom, and JoAnn Berry.

And for standing behind my paltry efforts at writing, these deserve special recognition: Linda Stanley, Verba Holly, Roffie Ensey, Pauline Elms, Margie McNall, Marilyn Zedlitz, Tonnie Greer, Karen Wehrle, Elaine Fauss, Kelly Daywitt, Mary Dean, Theresa Beasley, Ruby Krenek, Paula Battrell, Barbara Whitaker (my "sales manager"), and all the dear members of our church in Morris, Oklahoma.

Chapter One

Memory's Eddy

"Good afternoon, ma'am. Is the man of the house around?"

A long shadow stretched across the sun-baked earth to the east of the tall, statuesque man with hat in hand on the short front stoop.

Never let a stranger know you live alone.

Dessie hesitated, while three-year-old Becky clung to her skirt shyly.

"I've lost a wagon wheel," the gentleman hurried to explain. "The heat, I'm sure."

Dessie's eyes met the stranger's, and her heart gave an abrupt leap. It had been ten years since she had looked into those mahogany eyes. There could never be a duplicate of them, but even if there could, the one deep wave in the front of his hair and the hint of a cleft in his chin would have given him away. He did not recognize her, of course; for that she was grateful.

"There's an extra wheel in the shed out back, sir. I'm sure Walt wouldn't mind you using it."

"Thank you, ma'am. Tell the man I'll return it when I get mine repaired." He was gone, taking his infinite shadow with him.

I told the truth, Dessie reasoned. I'm sure Walt wouldn't mind *if he were alive.*

Dessie grasped the arm of the spider rocker and turned its oak back to the window, then yielded herself to its comforting support. Becky, fretting childishly, climbed onto her lap, and Dessie began to rock heedlessly.

What was Nathan Parsons doing in Limestone Gap? He had obviously traveled some distance in the searing summer heart. Was he just passing through? Something in his brunet eyes haunted her. Was it pain? bitterness? anger?

The backwash of time's flow pulled her into the eddy of memory . . . back past last year's tragedy to her girlhood days in the community of Brazos Point. She caught a reflection of herself, as clearly as the girl who looked in the mirror that afternoon ten years ago, dressed in her best calico dress, meticulously starched and ironed with the flat black iron. Her brother William teased her about her hair. "Gettin' mighty vain," he accused, bringing an unmistakable flush to her cheeks. Blushing was an error that brought more merciless ribbing.

"Mind yore own beeswax!" she retorted. She had piled her heavy bronze-colored hair atop her head in coils of curls to transform her just-turned-sixteen youthfulness to an appearance of maturity. All to impress Nathan Parsons.

"Parson Stevens got a preacher all th' way from Loosanna fer th' annual brush arbor meetin'," Henry Harris reported. "Got a right fetchin' laddy, too."

12

Dessie could see Nathan now in all his pre-twenty pomp, moving about easily, his gangling six-foot-two frame almost plunging his head of black hair into the swinging coal oil lanterns. He tuned his round-hole guitar by plunking a note on the ancient piano and adjusting the wooden tuning keys on his instrument by ear until the corresponding sound pleased him. Sister Myrt, the church's antiquated musician, frowned jealously.

Then he turned and looked directly at Dessie, grinning boyishly. She was smitten! Thereafter, he took her gaze—and heart—with him wherever he went. The preacher's eloquent sermon was wasted on her.

Funny the things one remembered about such isolated incidents. The stars, for instance. She recalled the buggy ride home from church that night. One particular star left its orbit to tail a white streak across the inky sky, then disappear into black oblivion. Now that she thought of it, it seemed prophetic of that one brilliant splash of romance in her lackluster teenage life.

"Th' preacher's son asked what yore name was," William tormented. "Mayhap he's sweet on ya."

Dessie glared at him. Another mistake. "Dessie's mad an' I'm glad an' I know what t' please 'er," he chanted.

Daydreams through a sleepless night, built of wishful thinking, took her deep into breathless anticipation of a protracted meeting that would last for weeks and weeks. This spine-tingling romance would go on forever and ever. . . .

Her infatuation lasted two nights. Before the third hand-clapping, foot-stomping service, Pastor Stevens sent word to his parishoners that a wire had come from Louisiana proclaiming a dire family emergency, taking evangelist and son back to the land of their beginnings. Dessie was left with an empty memory of a handsome guitar player.

"Gambler's luck, Dessie," William taunted. She turned her back to hide blinding tears.

She supposed that on the strength of that two-day acquaintance she would have followed him back to his native land and married him had he asked her to. That would have been a tragic mistake, of course, curtailing her education and forever erasing Walt from her future. Life without Walt? or Becky? or the Gap? She shuddered at the thought.

Walter diffused into her life as unobtrusively as a slow summer sunset. And as beautifully, she reflected. The whole community knew that love stalked her tracks before she did. She had finished school and taught for four years, supposing that matrimony had passed her by, pretending not to care. During these years, marrying Walter never once entered her thoughts.

Now in memory's wake, Dessie's mind could find no defined birth of the courtship. No wild fireworks of emotion or mad passion blighted their practical relationship. Throughout her growing-up years, he was simply *there*. At church. At parties. At weddings and funerals and baptizings. Like the Bible on the mantle. Something you saw every day, but somehow failed to appreciate or recognize its value, until one day you realized you needed the strength that only it could provide, and you found your comfort there.

Walter, a younger son of the large Gibson family from the nearby farm, was hailed as steady, trustworthy, and unworldly. He asked little of life save a sense of peace and harmony with himself and his fellow man. Undistinguished and commonplace, the local lasses passed him by for his illustrious counterparts.

Dessie's older sister, Sarah, wed Walter's older brother many years earlier, and they plugged out a comfortable living on their river-front acreage in the age-old pattern of earthly existence.

So it came as no surprise, but rather as a natural culmination, when Walter Gibson asked Henry Harris for his daughter's hand in marriage, promising to love her, cherish her, and forsake all others for her alone until death. And he could be depended on to do just that. Even the wedding, which took place in the Harris parlor, lacked resplendence.

"I been hopin' on anuther Gibson in th' bunch fer years, Dessie," her mother commented. "I'm pleased as a purrin' kitten."

The shock came when Walter loaded his wagon and left to make a life for himself and his bride outside Bosque County. "I want to provide something better for my bride than a shanty on the banks of the Brazos River," he said. No power could dissuade him from his decision.

He had read an advertisement for rock quarry workers in a remote place called Limestone Gap, and the wages staggered his imagination. With a flowing supply of cash, his Dessie could have life's niceties. And he existed for Dessie's happiness.

Thus, to the Gap—for that's what its residents called it—they moved, leaving the Harris and Gibson families to mourn their going.

"Joseph an' Amy moved 'way off to th' Territory, an' now Dessie's leavin' us, too," Martha fretted. "A fam'ly that scatters tatters, is what my maw always said."

"Dessie stayed longer'n most," reminded Henry, in his usual sanguine manner.

Before long the young couple had a good home, a milk cow, a buggy, and order-book furniture, plus the bonus of a little money in the bank.

"Now if God will just bless us with a child," Walter said, "our life will be complete."

Becky, Walter's pride and joy, arrived in the year that followed. He loved nothing better than returning from his shift in the quarry to find Dessie in her starched gingham apron, crooning lullabies to her tiny replica. "To ask for more from life would be sinful," he laughed. "I'm the richest man on earth!"

The end came so suddenly for Walt. The foreman sent someone to the house to inform Dessie of the accident and to convey his condolences. . . . A falling rock. . . .

A light knock on the door, scarcely audible, pulled Dessie from her reverie. She laid her sleeping child in her bed and tiptoed to answer the summons.

Fair-haired Lucy Wells handed a sealed envelope to Dessie. The shadow of her parasol made a long, distorted canopy along the ground. "Father asked me to bring you this note, Mrs. Gibson."

"Won't you come in, Lucy?" Dessie stepped aside to let Lucy enter.

"I'd best not, Mrs. Gibson. Thanks anyhow. Papa has a school board meeting at our house tonight, and I'm to help Mother with the refreshments." She excused herself with a polite little curtsy. The playful shadow bobbed along beside her as she hurried away, waving a cheerful goodbye.

16

Now what business could the honorable mayor of the Gap have in sending her a personal message? He and Walt were neighborly, but now that Walt was gone . . .

She reached for the sterling silver letter opener, a wedding gift from her thoughtful groom, and opened the note.

"Mrs. Gibson," it read, "I am soliciting your permission to present your name to the school board to fill a teaching vacancy in the Gap's school district. I understand that you have teaching experience and very high credentials. It would be an honor to have you on the staff." It was signed "Mayor Wells."

He had taken for granted that she would be interested in his offer and probably felt he was doing her a favor by providing her a job opportunity in Walt's absence. Of course, she could not—would not—accept such a position, not with a small child to care for. Walt would not have been happy with her leaving Becky with a nurse. The salary would be helpful, but with the small compensation from the quarry and the sum that Walt had left her in the bank, she could manage for a few weeks yet. Then she'd decide what to do.

Dessie knew she must get word to the mayor before the night's meeting. She threw a worried look at the banjo clock on the mantle. Mayor Wells must not be allowed to present her name as a possibility to the school board. She hastened to awake Becky, pulling the child's prettiest dress over the sleepy head.

Taking Becky's small hand, Dessie headed for the mayor's home, cutting across the pasture to gain time and distance. She pointed out her own long shadow and the child's shorter one to Becky, painfully missing Walt's shadow beside them. Pastor Stevens used to say heaven was a place without shadows. She hoped so.

Dessie was scarcely out of sight when Nathan Parsons swung his wagon through the gate to return the borrowed wheel.

Chapter Two

The Argument

"Soak them wagon wheels in th' river, Henry," Martha said. "Get 'um ready for th' long trip. I can't stand it no longer."

Tears like iridescent pearls still clung to Martha's gray lashes.

"When yore maw gits a hankerin' fer one o' her'n, talkin' jest blows through yore hat," Henry told fifteen-year-old Sally, the youngest of the Harris family.

The worn letter, soiled by handling and rumpled by many readings, lay on the quilt-box lid. The neat characters, lined like gallant soldiers in a row, marched across the pages with quiet dignity.

"Dessie's writin' could make th' cheapest tablet wish 'twas a king's scroll," Martha once said. And Henry was inclined to agree.

"Ifn th' rail went that direction, you'd be goin' to Limestone Gap ever' month," Henry commented dryly, "an' leavin' me a grass widderer."

"Yore prob'ly right, Henry. Yore prob'ly right."

"But it'll be many a year afore th' iron horse runs to that remote a place, I'm afeared. They gotta keep th' trains goin' to big places like Dallas an' Independence an' Santa Fe."

"How fer did ya figger 'twas from here t' there, Henry?"

"Beats a hundred mile by my calculatin'."

"A measly hunderd mile can't keep me away from my grievin' girl."

"It's pow'rful hot to go right now, Martha. Can't you see fittin' to wait a month er so more?"

"I feel it here, Henry." Martha laid her work-worn hand on her bosom. "Dessie an' th' baby needs me. Now."

Henry had learned the futility of disputing a mother's intuition. He might as well start soaking the wooden wheels for the trip.

"Who all er goin'?" he asked. "You goin', Sally?"

"Do I hafta, Mama?" Sally turned imploring eyes toward Martha. "I jest hate ridin' fer long, 'specially when it's so terrible hot."

"Will ya mind William ifn I leave you?"

"Ifn he ain't too unreason'ble. Bossin' goes to his head when you ain't around."

"I don't want you makin' eyes at no menfolks whiles I'm away . . ."

"Aw, Mama. Jest cause Sarah married early, ain't no sign I gotta. I'm gonna be like Dessie an' wait til I'm twenty-two! Now Dessie was *smart.*"

"Jest be shore you don't forget that little resolution when a romeo-in' lad comes 'long." Martha faced Henry, her voice firm with decision. "Henry, I'm gonna let 'er stay. I wanna go as empty as possible 'cause I'm feelin' like Dessie's gonna wanna come back home with us'ns. What call is there fer 'er to stay out there in them wilds all alone with Walt gone an' none o' 'er fam'ly to see after 'er welfare 'er holp 'er?"

"Did she make mention o' comin' back with us'ns in th' letter?"

"No, but I read lonesome 'tween ever' line o' this letter." Martha patted the wrinkled paper.

"An' I hear lon'some 'tween ever' word you say," added Henry wryly. "Ifn you have yore way, Martha, she'll be returnin' on our wagen."

"I 'spect she could git 'er old teachin' job back at th' Brazos Point school right easy-like. None o' th' younguns, er even th' trustees, likes Miz Cowan as well as they did our Dessie. Our Dessie's jest a *special* kind o' teacher. They could transfer Miz Cowan over to th' Springs. She wouldn't mind none atall. Why, I heard 'er say with my own ears that she'd druther teach in a bigger place. We're too country to suit 'er fancy."

"Dessie might not be happy to leave 'er little 'un an work."

"With me she wouldn't mind none. She wouldn't want to leave 'er baby with nobody else, shore." Martha sighed wearily. "Henry, it's been more'n a year since I seen little Becky. An' now to think th' little darlin' ain't got no Paw . . ." Fresh tears threatened to splash over the already red rims of her eyelids. "I knowed they shouldn't't'a went off into that awful fersaken place. I tried my best to tell 'em. I heared all my life that th' quarry was a turrible danger'us place fer to work."

"Martha, Walt coulda got hisself killed right here afarmin' ifn 'twas 'is time to meet 'is Maker."

21

"I don't b'lieve he would'ave, though. There's sech a thang as an untimely death, Henry. I heared Brother Stevens mention it in a sermon onct. Leastwise ifn Walt'd'a been here, we'd'a been by our Dessie to comfort 'er in 'er sorrow at th' buryin' an' laid 'im away by th' rest o' our departed 'uns 'stead o' hearin' 'bout it a week later!"

Martha made hasty preparations to leave, driven by her motherly concern. She limited the baggage to scarcely more than the clothes they would need for the journey, conserving the space for Dessie's things. "How long'll it take us, Henry?"

"Five, maybe six days, travelin' light as we are. That's if'n we don't have no troubles o' no kind."

"We'll ask the Lord's smiles," Martha remarked.

Strange inns and strange beds along the way further subtracted from Martha's tranquility, but comforts were forgotten in her frantic determination to reach Dessie. "I should'a come afore now," she pressed. "'Cept I couldn't leave Sarah in 'er long-time confinement. Jest think, Henry. Dessie's been widdered quite a spell now. Th' poor, poor darlin'."

Martha managed to strike up a conversation with any proprietor's wife, cook, or livery boy along the route who would give her an audience.

"We're headed way out to Limestone Gap," she explained time and again. "To see our grievin' daughter what lost 'er husband in a quarry accident. A rock fell on 'is head . . . She has one little 'un. We're hopin' she'll come on back home with us to th' farm, seein's she don't have nobody to holp 'er out there . . ."

Some of her listeners were sympathetic; others merely nodded, seeking escape from the unsolicited story.

At daybreak each day of the trip, she rushed Henry through his coffee-drinking and visiting, anxious to reach Dessie and the child. "Can't waste no daylight time, Henry. Let's be out an' movin'." But for her impatience, Henry would have enjoyed the tour.

Her obsession to talk about Dessie accelerated with the miles. The shorter the distance, the longer the talks. "Henry, ain't life queer-like?"

"What you meanin' by that, Martha?"

"Take our Dessie fer instance. Fer years an' years she never married. I thought she was gonna be a spinster shore. She didn't even seem innerested in a husband. Then when she does finally git 'er a good man, she don't git to keep 'im long."

"I 'spect she'd druther had 'im fer four year than none atall, Martha. After all, she has Becky now."

"But Dessie was always so *unselfish,* Henry. Remember how she used to share with little crippled-up Effie?"

"Yep. Dessie always had a good heart inside 'er. But it rains on th' just an' th' unjust outta th' same sky like I always said."

"An' as fer as I knowed, Walter is th' onliest beau Dessie ever had in 'er whole life through. She jest wadn't taken up with th' boys like other girls was."

"I only remember one other'n."

"There wadn't no 'nother one, Henry. What you meanin'?"

"Do you remember th' arbor revival we had th' year Matthew got married? Lemme see now, that must'a been th' summer o' '91 . . ."

"Th' protracted meetin' that shut down 'cause th' preacher had sick folks back home in Loosanna?"

"That 'un."

"I remember. But what's that to do with th' subject we was talkin' on 'bout Dessie?"

"Th' preacher had a lad."

Martha furrowed her brow.

"Remember, he was a good-lookin', late-teenish boy what played th' geetar right nice-like an' Dessie took a shine to 'im."

"Aw, Henry, that was jest puppy love. She never even talked to th' fellar to my recollectin'. Dessie warn't but scant sixteen. Sixteen's too young fer *real* love."

"Why, Martha, you was sixteen when we got married. Was it real love, 'er jest puppy love?" Henry's eyes twinkled with mischief; to catch Martha in her words amused him.

"But Henry," objected Martha, "back then it was different. We was lots more growed up at sixteen. I always figgered th' war 'tween th' states made our generation mature faster. Nowadays sixteen-year-olds er still *children.*"

"Sarah fell in love with Hank at sixteen."

"Well, Henry, I don't know what yore tryin' to prove by yore arguments, but Dessie shore warn't innerested in that boy—what was 'is name?"

"Parsons. Nathan Parsons."

"That's right. I recollect now. Parsons. They only stayed two nights, an' can't nobody git innerested in somebody in jest two short nights. Anyhow have you ever heared 'er mention 'is name a'onct since that day ten year ago?"

"No, but I found 'is name writ on th' back o' th' barn with chalk."

"Who writ it?"

"Looked mighty like Dessie's writin'."

"Prob'ly William's! William always loved ribbin' an' rilin' 'er any way he could."

"Th' rain warshed it off an' she writ it back agin."

"Puppy love."

"It said, 'Dessie claims Nathan ferever.'"

"Ferever, ha. An' I dare say she ain't never given 'im anuther thought in 'er whole life from that day till this!"

"She shore waited a pow'rful long time afore she finally jumped th' broom with Walt."

"Dessie's jest not natured of bein' flirtatious, Henry. I don't 'spect she'll ever marry agin now that she's lost Walt."

"Likely not."

The wagon wheel on Martha's side jostled against a boulder, causing her to grapple for support and sidetracking her thoughts, but Henry smiled on.

Chapter Three

The Returned Wheel

"*P*apa will see you in five minutes, Mrs. Gibson." Lucy's curls sprang as she talked. "He had an unexpected guest that just left."

"Thank you, Lucy. I'll wait."

Dessie sat on the padded deacon's bench in the parlor, holding Becky on her lap. She had never been inside the mayor's well furnished home, proclaimed to be the most exclusive in the township, but Walt had described it to her.

Had she sat here a few months ago, before Walt's passing, she would have surveyed the rich surroundings with insatiable interest. The ornate old organ, obviously a family heirloom, with its treadles worn thin in a foot-shaped pattern would have intrigued her, as well as the oval picture frames encircling portraits of stern-looking relatives that graced the tall walls.

But now none of this earthly trivia mattered. The ache of loneliness that gnawed at her consciousness could never be assuaged with mere *things*, however expensive. Without the warmth of a human element, inanimate ob-

jects were useless, often even tiresome. She pulled Becky
closer to her breast and kissed her soft hair, grateful for
a warm little body to hold near her.

"I'll see you now, Mrs. Gibson. And I hope you'll pardon the delay."

Dessie lifted Becky to the floor, caught her chubby
hand, and walked into the plush library, feeling vaguely
out of place but obediently taking the chair that Mayor
Wells indicated.

"Lucy delivered my note to you?"

"Yes, sir."

"I hope you have come with an affirmative answer
for me to present to the board tonight."

"I'm afraid that would be quite impossible, sir."

"Oh, I'm sure it wouldn't," contradicted Mr. Wells
cheerfully, accustomed to bending circumstances to his
liking. "We'll just see what we can do to make it possible. We feel, of course, that the salary is quite enviable
for a woman. Walt was a good friend of mine. He voted
for me as mayor, and I feel I'm doing a favor to his
memory to place you first on the list of prospective
teachers for our school. I can pull strings and get you the
job. Good jobs for women are scarce in these remote
areas."

"I thank you for your consideration, Mr. Wells, but
I wouldn't be interested in the teaching position."

"I understand that you have taught before."

"Yes, sir. For four years."

"Did you enjoy teaching, Mrs. Gibson?"

"Oh, very much, sir. Each of my pupils was special
to me. I still get letters from some of them. When Walt
died, I was swamped with notes of sympathy . . ."

"You admit you love teaching. You say you have experience. So your hesitancy to accept our offer makes no sense." He possessed a politician's gift of persuasion.

Dessie smiled and nodded toward Becky. "I have a child now."

"That's one more reason why you *should* teach, my dear lady," Mr. Wells pointed out patiently. "To be better able to provide for your child's future needs."

"I . . . I'm afraid I couldn't bring myself to leave her."

"I'm sure you could find someone responsible . . ."

"I'm sure I could, sir. But I wouldn't."

Mr. Wells stopped and pondered. Dessie Gibson had her mind made up, and it would be futile to try to dissuade this young widow. Her sorrow had cut deep, and sensitive scabs remained. He decided on another tactic. He couldn't let a teacher with these qualifications slip from his grasp. He had the education of his own Lucy to consider.

He dipped his pen into the inkwell and wrote on a pad. "I'll talk to the board of directors tonight, Mrs. Gibson. It may be that we can work out a plan to allow you to take the child into the classroom with you. She seems well behaved." He gave Becky a conspiratorial wink. "Of course, it's against state regulations, but we here at the Gap are known to run our affairs to our own liking and keep our mouths shut about it. We might have to hide her when the county superintendent comes by, but that wouldn't be very often. If I can persuade the board to hire you with your little assistant here, would you consider teaching our school next semester? We have found no one that can touch your credentials."

Dessie sat in thoughtful silence. Decision day could not be postponed indefinitely. She had known all along that she would have to do something with her life—either return to Brazos Point to her parents' home or supplement her income in this forsaken land.

Here she had her home. Here she had Walt's grave. Here she could live independently, burdening no one. The thought of moving back into her parents' home disconcerted her. Once one left home to make a life of one's own, one never quite fit back into the pattern.

And what about Becky? Grandparents tended to spoil children devoid of a parent. And yet, to deny a child the love of caring grandparents could be unwise, too. She had sorely missed having a grandmother herself and envied her classmates when they told of weekends spent with these special guardians.

What did the future hold for her here in the Gap? But for that matter, what did the future hold for her in the community of her birth? On the ledger of minuses and pluses, the columns seemed fairly equal.

Mr. Wells adjusted his spectacles and cleared his throat. Dessie realized that she was being unfair to keep him waiting, especially since he had a board meeting that night.

"Please give me time to think it over, sir."

Mr. Wells frowned. It would mean calling another tedious board meeting at which no one could agree upon anything. On the other hand, it had been a sudden proposal for the young widow. It would only be logical and fair to grant her time to adjust to the idea of returning to work. She had had a four-year reprieve. Of course, when she considered the pros and cons, she would concede. Negative thoughts were foreign to Mr. Wells.

"Could you perhaps give us a definite decision within

a week, Mrs. Gibson?"

"Yes, sir, I think so."

Mrs. Wells came with dainty teacakes and demitasse cups of black coffee, some of the refreshments Lucy spoke of preparing for tonight's meeting. Becky ate with gusto, licking icing from her fingers gingerly while Dessie kept a nervous watch on the sinking sun. As soon as propriety allowed, she dismissed herself.

Dessie started back across the pasture. The shadows stretched very long now and were directly in front of her, giving her the eerie sensation that they were leading instead of following.

"I didn't know we'd be gone so long," she said to the child. "I didn't close up the house." It was spoken as a statement rather than a worry. No one had ever bothered anything; few people even knew where she lived.

She began thinking about the teaching job. Perhaps it would answer an inner need. She would have less time for meditation, active children for companionship (for herself and Becky), and an income besides. With extra money, she could take Becky on a coach to visit the home place on holidays, or she might be brave enough to buy herself a "newfangled horseless carriage" if they proved as reliable as the newspapers professed them to be. She laughed to think what Martha's reaction would be to that idea.

And then, hadn't she asked God to direct her future? Could this be an answer to prayer?

Deep in thought, Dessie's eyes saw the wheel leaned against the side of the house without seeing it with her mind.

"A wheel, Mommy!" Becky pointed out, and Dessie

stared at it in alarm.

Someone had been here. Someone had left the wheel standing against the wall. The note tucked in the screen caught her attention. Scrawled unevenly in a man's hasty handwriting, it said: "Dear Sir: I returned your wagon wheel. Much obliged. Perhaps I can return the favor some day." It was signed "D. Parsons."

She had missed him! Her heart constricted with a sudden wave of disappointment. But why should she care?

Chapter Four

Martha's Proposal

"*I* shore don't like this part o' th' country, Henry," Martha frowned as the terrain developed deep washes and towers of jutting rock. "It looks plum' frightful."

"We'd'a shore throwed a rim ifn we hadn't soaked th' wheels goodly. I'm thinkin' we're gettin' nigh on to Limestone Gap."

"Seein' th' countryside makes me pure determined to get our Dessie outta here!"

The Gap nestled in a natural oasis fed by an orphan stream and flanked by rocky foothills. From any given direction, one came upon it quite unexpectedly, and its facade was equally as surprising. Besides the thriving rock quarries, a textile mill kept its pulse beating.

"Why look, Martha!" Henry articulated. "It's bigger'n our own town!"

Martha, taken aback, and not wishing to be favorably impressed, muttered, "An' likely wickeder, too."

Dessie, gazing out her window in prayerful meditation about the teaching position while Becky napped, saw the familiar Harris wagon pull into the yard and ran to meet it joyfully, hairpins flying from her loose chignon.

"Mama!" she cried. "What a lovely surprise!" She fell into Martha's outstretched arms. After the tearful embrace, Martha held her at arm's length to study her facial features. The grief had certainly not diminished her youthful beauty. Gold flecks still gilded her emerald eyes and the burnished shock of hair complemented her smooth, tawny complexion.

"Yore certainly lookin' well, Dessie."

"God has been my refuge and my fortress, Mama."

"We shore prayed fer you."

"I could feel those prayers, and I thank you."

"How's our littl'un?"

"She's managing better than her mother. She's too young to really realize her loss. She fretted for Walt for a few days, but the forgetfulness of babyhood has already begun its work. She'll never really remember her daddy . . ."

"I hope you have a good picture of 'im to show her."

"No, Mama, I don't have. Having Walt in person seemed enough. I'm afraid I simply took life for granted. It's ironic. Walt came into my life so slowly and left so suddenly."

They walked toward the house. The sun slipped behind a summer cloud, eliminating the shadows.

"What's this wagon wheel doin' just leanin' agin' th' house here, Dessie?" asked Henry, kicking at the wooden spoke with the toe of his hightopped shoe. "Someun lost it?"

"No, it belongs to me, Papa," Dessie turned her face away when she felt the color rising to her cheeks. "I

34

loaned it to a friend who returned it yesterday, and I just haven't put it back in the shed."

"I'll tote it back fer you."

"There's no rush." She said it quickly, unpremeditated. "Come on in and peek at Becky. I think she makes an angelic picture when she's sleeping."

Martha observed Dessie closely, relieved that she had apparently escaped the ravages of bitterness. Dessie had always "Faced hardness as a good soldier," but when it came to parting with one's beloved companion, the mettle was tried to the limits of endurance.

"I jest got to yearnin' to see you an' Becky," explained Martha. "I felt like you might be lonesome out here all by yoreself."

"It has been hard, Mama. And lonely. Without Becky, I don't know how I could have stood it."

"Yore not plannin' on stayin' on here in this fersaken place, er you, Dessie?" The tight-strung words bounced from Martha's compressed emotions.

"I . . . really haven't quite decided what I'm going to do . . ."

"Walt wouldn't fault you none fer leavin' his grave an' goin' back to fam'ly an' friends. 'Tisn't him here no more nohow; his spirit's done moved to heaven."

"An' you'll have to have some kind o' income, Dessie." Henry tacked on his addendum. "Less'n you come live with us."

"Walt left me a little money in the bank, but I know it won't last indefinitely. I've been offered a teaching job here in the Gap . . ."

"But Dessie!" cautioned Martha. "You shore wouldn't think o' leavin' yore onliest baby with a nursemaid! Why,

I couldn't sleep nary a wink at night knowin' . . .''

"No, Mama, I wouldn't leave Becky. That's settled."

"An' you shore couldn't take 'er to school with you."

"It's against the school policy, but it seems they're so desperate for teachers in this area that the mayor is willing to try to bend the rules to allow me to take her to classes with me."

"'Tain't at all necessary, Dessie. We have that big old house with only Arthur an' Sally still yet home, an' you can move right back into yer old room. Ifn you want to teach to fill up th' heart-hurtin' hours, I'll be more'n delighted to keep an eye on little Becky fer you. Sally's a great hand with younguns 'erself. Pay might not be as good there, but expenses would be lesser by a fer piece."

"Maw come after you, Dessie!" laughed Henry. "Can't you tell? You might as well start barrelin' up yore b'longins."

"What would I do about my house and furniture here?"

"You can publish 'em in th' paper fer sale." Martha had a ready answer. "We'll stay till you rid yore mind o' th' property."

Martha's proposal made sense on the surface. What reason had a young widow to live miles away from any family member, holding onto a shadow of the past? If make a living for herself she must, she could as easily teach school in familiar surroundings, tutoring children of families she had known all her life. Death severed any obligation that she might have to maintain a home in this wilderness.

"I tole Paw," Martha was saying when Dessie reined her attention back to the conversation, "that you was so long in marryin' that I 'spected you'd never marry agin nohow."

"I have no plans of remarrying."

"Won't never be another Walt."

"Truer words were never spoken, Mama."

"Yore Papa and me had a discussion comin' down 'bout you an' Walter."

"More like an argument," interspersed Henry with chagrin.

"I contended that Walter was yore one an' onliest beau an' yore Paw contends different."

"Who won the debate?" queried Dessie.

"Neither'n, I guess you'd say."

"You remember that travelin preacher's boy what came to th' arbor meetin' th' year Matthew 'n Pauline married?"

Dessie gave a muffled cough. "That was ancient history, Papa."

"I tole you she wouldn't even remember 'is name, Henry." Martha addressed Dessie, "Paw said you carried a torch in yore heart fer th' boy, but I said 'twarn't nought but puppy love, ifn 'twas anything atall, seein's you was so youngish."

Dessie looked away. "There's several kinds and degrees of love, I suppose," she mused, "and a heart is adaptable."

"But yer love fer Walt was th' only real one."

"Yes, my love for Walt was real." Dessie clasped her fingers together. "It wasn't the dizzy, heart-spinning kind, but it was solid and comforting, and everything anyone could ask of a marriage. It would have been a mistake to marry anyone else."

"Now you see, Henry, I won th' argument . . . as usual."

Dessie back-tracked the discourse to see how much Henry recalled. "What *was* the young man's name, Papa?" Of course he was talking about Nathan.

"'Twas Nathan Parsons. Th' way I recollect was somebody writ his name on th' back o' th' barn."

He looked at Dessie quickly, searchingly. She swallowed hard and breathed a sign of relief when Becky stirred, diverting Henry and Martha's attention.

"But you *will* consider goin' back home with us to Brazos Point, won't you, Dessie?"

"I'll pray about it, Mama," Dessie promised.

Before going to sleep, she took Nathan's scribbled note from between the pages of her Bible and read it again. Closing her eyes, she became a girl again, zealously writing the message on the barn in bold letters. She had loved Nathan Parsons . . . with all the fervor of her sixteen-year-old being.

But no doubt Nathan was married and had a family of his own by now. She puzzled over his signature. Why had he signed it *D*. Parsons?

She replaced the paper . . . after one dizzy, head-spinning flashback.

Chapter Five

The Strange Dream

"*P*aw thinks you oughtta put yore property into th' hands o' a seller an' us start back to th' farm tomorra," Martha relayed on the third morning of the visit. Her eyes roamed about the room, separating the things to be taken from those to be left behind.

Dessie knew that Henry, a home-natured soul, could not be held away from his magnetic forty acres for long. The miracle was, she decided, that Martha persuaded him to venture off the home place at all.

In his hours of restlessness, Henry had grubbed stumps, repaired the sagging shed door, and whittled out a toy duck for Becky. But when he started to move the wagon wheel leaning against the outside wall back to its place in the shed, Dessie objected. "Just leave it there, Papa. My friend might come by needing it again."

"As you say, Dessie."

Becky wasted no time "heart-cuffing" both her grandparents with her charms, and Martha shrewdly concocted bedtime stories of good times the child could expect on the Harris farm. Dessie smiled at her mother's transparent motives, feeling much like a piece of floating balsam carried along the rushing stream of life toward a Brazos Point harbor, willing or not.

There was no need fighting Mama, Papa, and Becky. So she pulled a sheet of note paper from the walnut stationary and sat down to write the mayor, explaining her hasty exit and expressing her regret. The words would not come, however, so she shoved the paper back into the pigeonhole and prepared for a hurried trip to the real estate agent.

"Where ya goin', Dessie?" Henry asked.

"To Mr. Davis's office. He sells property for people, and I've heard he's a fair seller."

"I'll take you."

"It's not but a mile, and I need the exercise."

"Not in this kind o' heat."

Dessie laughed, comprehending his need to be busy and useful, but warned, "You'll just have to sit and wait for me, I'm afraid, Papa."

"I'll fetch me a sody at th' sody fountain an' plague th' sody jerk," he grinned. "There's always somethin' to do with a body's self!"

Dessie walked down the boardwalk of Main Street with her head erect, feeling curious eyes upon her. Few women negotiated business on Main Street. An eager-eyed man gazed her direction, and she hastened her steps. The sanctum of the crude office provided a welcomed shelter.

"What can I do for you, young lady?" The man behind the desk had graying hair and an honest face.

"You're . . . Mr. Davis?"

40

"Oscar Davis, ma'am."

"I'd like to sell my place."

"Selling out, huh?"

"Yes, sir. I'm returning to my birthplace."

"Don't like the Gap?"

"Oh, that's not the problem, sir!" Dessie lowered her eyes. "I . . . just have no family here and no reason to stay."

"I see." The man picked up a detailed document. "Your name?"

"Dessie Gibson."

"You must be . . . Walt Gibson's widow."

"Yes, sir. You knew him?"

"One of the finest men I ever met."

"Thank you, sir."

"We hate to see you leave our community, Mrs. Gibson."

"I don't see that it could possibly make any difference to you or the community, sir."

"It does, in fact. I'm on the school board, and we had hoped very much to have you for a teacher in our school this fall. You have excellent references."

Dessie blushed. It occurred to her that she should have broken the news to the mayor first. Now she would have to go directly from here to explain to the city's highest officer lest he hear the news and think ill of her for not notifying him of her decision first as she had promised.

"I . . . thank you." Did that make sense? She hoped it did; Mr. Davis had complimented her.

"The house will be unfurnished?"

"My furniture goes with it, sir. At least most of it. I have no way of taking anything except my personal belongings and a few sentimental pieces with me."

"Are you sure you are doing the right thing, Mrs. Gibson?" Mr. Davis dropped his pen and looked into her eyes.

"I . . . hope so."

"I hate to see a widow make a decision such as you are making. I find they sometimes regret it later. Will you be purchasing property there?"

"No, sir. I'll live with my parents, a sister, and a brother."

Mr. Davis shook his head. "I wish I could talk you out of it, Mrs. Gibson. You should give yourself more time. But of course, if you insist, I'm at your service."

"We'll be leaving sometime tomorrow."

"Let's see now." Mr. Davis retrieved his pen. "Your property adjoins the mayor's on one corner."

"The southwest."

"You have a good location, but property is selling poorly just now. It may be several weeks—or even months—before we have a nibble."

"I see."

"I did have a gentleman in today, however, interested in property in these parts. Name of Parsons. I didn't have anything on my listing that interested him, but I can mention your place to him when he checks back with me . . . if he ever does. Might be a sale; he wanted on the outskirts with a little land."

Parsons. Dessie's heart stood still. Could it be Nathan? Mr. Davis said he had been in *this* office today. This being the case, he might still be in town! An ulcerous fear gnawed at the lining of her mind. What if Henry ran across Nathan Parsons . . . and recognized him?

"Is something wrong, Mrs. Gibson?" solicited the

42

realtor.

"No, I . . ."

"Are you very sure this is what you want to do?"

"Yes. I'll leave my address, and you can let me know," Dessie heard herself saying in a recorded-cylinder tone as she arose to go, handing Mr. Davis a card on which she had printed the Brazos Point route. The room had suddenly become too small, and her foremost desire was to escape its confines.

She found her father in the drugstore, chatting amiably with an old-timer. "I hate to rush you, Papa, but I have another stop to make," she urged. "And if I'm to pack tonight, we must finish our business posthaste."

When Henry let her out at the mayor's house, she insisted that he go on to her house with a message for Martha to pack her pink cherry blossom dishes, a wedding gift from Walt's family, in the potato barrel. "I'll cut across the pasture and go the back way home when I'm done talking with Mr. Wells," she told him. "We have to make every minute count, you know."

Mr. Wells greeted her cordially, his optimism evident. "Well, well, our new teacher cometh!" he chuckled.

Before she had time to give her planned speech, he continued, "I want to tell you exactly what happened at that board meeting, Mrs. Gibson. It called for all the diplomacy I could muster! I laid the cards before the gentlemen, giving the simple, straight facts. 'Our prospective teacher has a small child,' I told them, 'and she wishes to take the child to class with her.' Some asked how old the tyke was, and others referred to the policy. It was tit for tat for about an hour, and on the first vote the majority was against taking you. I anticipated this, but I knew I held the winning card and then I made my speech, telling them what a tragic mistake they were making. 'That young widow can teach better with one hand holding a child's,' said I, 'than any of your other applicants can teach with both hands empty.' Someone eventually made a motion that we vote over again . . ." Mr. Wells stopped to chuckle at his own ingenuity. "The second vote was almost unanimous in your favor!"

"But I . . ."

"We won't have any problem locally. Our thorn in the flesh will be the new county superintendent. I don't like his attitude. He's cocky and carries a chip on his shoulder. Frankly, I don't know how he ever got the job, anyhow. I can tell you now that he and I will strike fire sooner or later. He lives several miles from here, thank goodness, and we'll only see him on rare occasions. The rarer, the better. He has about fifteen rural schools under his jurisdiction, so he'll be busy. I anticipate a run-in with him if he ever discovers the child in the classroom."

"I came to tell you . . ."

"Don't worry, Mrs. Gibson. I'm ready to defend you. The whole Limestone Gap school board is. We're ready for the city and county to lock horns. If it wasn't on this issue, it would be on something else. If I'm worth my salt as mayor of this city, we'll win. If I'm not, then I deserve to lose. I'll have to say I'm *glad* you have granted us the opportunity to controvert policy. The challenge intrigues me! I want to personally thank you." The mayor extended his hand.

A flustered Dessie, unable to get a word in edgewise, decided to write the note after all and put it in the mailbox before she left. It might be the coward's way out, she told herself, but her tongue refused to make the necessary resignation. And Mayor Wells refused to give it an opportunity.

She headed pensively across the pasture toward the house that had been her home for five years—the house that might some day belong to a man named Parsons.

Discolored blades of grass mingled with summer's green like Henry's telltale strands of gray hair among the dark. Autumn approached. She would not have to face the dreaded winter alone.

A buff-colored rabbit, scared from its brushy abode, ran in front of Dessie, uncertain which way to go for safety. It looked ahead, then back from where it had come, and at last decided to return to its familiar habitat.

That night Dessie dreamed she was the rabbit, standing in the middle of the road looking ahead to Brazos Point and back to the Gap. At last she turned back to the Gap, and the dream faded into a crescent of beautiful rainbows.

A New Idea

"*N*ow hadn't Dessie always been th' strangest child you ever saw, Henry?" Martha broke her morose silence, her voice as empty as the wagon that took her homeward. Henry wondered which disturbed her worse—that she didn't want to return home without Dessie or that Dessie didn't want to return home with her.

Henry, simply happy to be going back to his domicile, shrugged. "I don't see that she's so strange, Martha."

"At th' very last minnit, after we'd a'ready packed half 'er b'longins, she got her head sot agin' movin' back home with us where she b'longs. I can't fer th' life o' me figger it. I thought all time she was agreeable to returnin'."

"I'm not surprised."

"I guess you an' Dessie jest thank alike, Henry, I'm shore I don't understand her reasonin' no more'n I understand yourn most times. Seems to me th' sensible thang fer 'er to 'adone would'a been to come back to 'er family . . ."

"Martha, let me ask you one question." His tone carried a patience-in-tribulation note.

"Ask on."

"Ifn I was to die an' leave you a widder, would you be persuaded to up an' sell our home place an' go live with someone else, even ifn it 'twas family?"

"Why, no siree, Henry! Certainly not! I'd as soon die as do that! You know I'd never ever sell off th' homestead. What's th' matter with yore thankin'?" Martha failed to interpret Henry's obvious parable.

"Then why do you 'spect outta yore own childern somethin' you yoreself would never do?"

"But Henry! It's different . . ."

"Ain't no different. You don't give yore own childern th' same rights as you give yoreself. An' 'tain't fair. Not one bit. Like you hittin' th' ceilin' when Sarah got 'erself married off at th' very same age as what you did. Seems to me you have one set o' rules fer yore childern that's plum' different from th' rules you live by yoreself. An' with raisin' childern, a double standard don't work. My pappy always told me chickens come home to roost. 'Twas his way o' sayin' you reap yore own doin's sooner er later."

"But thank on little Becky, Henry. She'll have to be raised out in that there wilderness away from us'ns . . ."

"I'm afeared our motives er purely selfish, Martha. We wanted 'er nearby us when all th' time Limestone Gap was Dessie's home. She has 'er pretty furniture she'd'a had to give up, an' 'er nice house . . ."

"An' th' ole wagon wheel she won't let nobody touch!" Martha flung. "There was somethin' mighty 'spicious 'bout that wheel, ifn you ask me."

"Why, Martha . . ."

"She kept sayin' leave it be, 'cause her friend might come back needin' to borrow it agin. Now tell me, Henry Harris, do you think that friend was a *woman?*"

"Martha!"

"How many women drive wagons?"

"You have no call to think ill thoughts. So what ifn it 'twas a man. Neighbors can be friends."

"Henry, Dessie's a lone woman. An' lone women are so . . . so *defenseless.*"

"Don't be fretsome, Martha. She has some pow'rful good neighbors. Th' mayor won't let nuthin' happen to harm her er Becky."

"An' with you not likin' to travel . . . it'll be eternities afore I git to go see her an' my gran'baby agin."

"Dessie said she'd ride th' stage to see us on holidays."

"I'm jest worried sick over 'er, Henry. 'Tis th' mother in me. An' I can't hep it."

"No need troublin' trouble till trouble troubles you, Martha. Jest pray."

"Winter's comin' on afore long, too, Henry."

"She'll make it, Martha."

"She needs someone to do the *man* work. She ain't strong enough to chop wood an' haul ice-crusted water."

"She can hire it done."

"Henry, I can't b'lieve a father so unconcerned as you. Why, you know she'd not have th' money to hire a wood cutter an' a water hauler an' a fence fixer, an' all."

"I don't know what you expect me to do, Martha. We can't desert th' rest o' th' family an' come live with 'er. We still yet have two o' ourn at home, remember—Sally an' Arthur. An' you jest seen that we can't convince 'er to come live with us."

Martha brooded past patches of plants of the crowfoot family, their irregular blooms wilting in the late summer temperature. The flora, with the huddles of head-high brake, did not interest her; her shoulders slumped with misgivings. Henry drove on, ignoring her melancholy slough of desond.

Suddenly she straightened, a gleam of victory in her steel-gray eyes. "I have an idee, Henry!"

"Watch out 'bout them idees, Martha. The last 'un didn't work out too well."

"But this 'un will. Even you'll thank so. You'll see."

"Speak it up."

"When we get back to Brazos Point, we'll send Arthur out on th' coach to stay th' winter with Dessie. He can do th' man work like choppin' an' haulin' wood. An' he can protect 'er, too. That way, I wouldn't be so inclined to fret so 'bout Dessie."

"Now, Martha, that is a good idee. A very good 'un. I wisht you always thought discernin' like that. Arthur's right handy."

"You can crop without 'im this year, can't you, Henry?"

"Yep. Th' other boys'd come over an' help me ifn they knowed Arthur was helpin' their widdered sister. William 'specially."

"An' besides, it'll do Arthur good. He's restless. He's turnin' twenty an' gettin' kinda itchy to see another part o' th' world. I don't want 'im hikin' off unannounced like Joseph did."

"You ain't jest tryin' to get Arthur away from Shada

50

Moore, er you, Martha?"

"Honest, Henry, I never gave that one little thought. I was truly thinkin' on Dessie's welfare."

"You don't s'pose Dessie would mind?"

"No, Dessie wouldn't mind. She has th' extry lean-to room that we stayed in."

"An' they always got along a heap better'n William an' Sally."

"She'll love havin' Arthur to help 'er since she'll be teachin' school. She always favored Arthur. An' besides, it'll take away Dessie's lonesome."

"You don't think it'd be better to send Sally so's Dessie could have some girl company?"

"No, Dessie needs a man 'round th' place. She has th' mayor's girl fer girl company right next over. Anyways, I couldn't part with Sally. I'd ferever be afeared Dessie'd let 'er make eyes at th' boys at school. Sally needs a heavy hand. An' Sally don't like to travel b'sides."

"I jest hope Arthur'll agree. We're gettin' ourselves mighty hoped up afore we consult 'im."

"Oh, he will. He'll be rarin' to go th' minnit we mention it! He'll be checkin' to see when the next coach leaves."

"D'ya thank we ort to send Dessie a wire that Arthur's comin'?"

"No, I don't thank so. She might get a notion in 'er head that she was misputtin' us an' try to talk me outta my idee, an' I know it's what we had ort to do."

"As you say, Martha."

Chapter Seven

Arthur's Arrival

*D*essie, her unwavering decision reached, set about to make a new wardrobe of "teaching" dresses on her sewing apparatus. Stamina gradually seeped back into her sorrowing heart, replenishing the loveliness of womanhood.

"I'm glad you'll be teaching in our school, Mrs. Gibson." Since the appointment, Lucy Wells visited often, counting the diminishing days until school's onset. Her sweet innocence crowned perfect features.

"I'm glad, too." Dessie filled the long bobbin with green thread.

"I was afraid you'd decide to go back home with your mother."

"I considered it, Lucy. I had almost decided to go, but then I had a strange thing happen that changed my mind."

"Would I be rude to ask what it was?"

"It was a dream."

"Do you believe dreams mean something, Mrs. Gibson?"

"Most of them don't, but once in a while they do. I knew when I awoke that this one did."

"I wish I could tell when they have a meaning and when they don't."

Dessie laughed. "Are you a dreamer?"

"Yes, I dream most every night. Sometimes I don't remember what I dream, but when I awoke this morning, I recalled last night's dream quite clearly."

"I hope it wasn't about the county superintendent pitching me out!"

"No, it was a good dream. I dreamed that a young man with dark hair, brown eyes, and wearing a blue shirt came and took me away on his horse. The dream ended in rainbows."

Rainbows. Her own dream had faded into rainbows. "It's unusual to dream in color," Dessie said.

"It's the first time I ever remember dreaming of a rainbow."

"I've dreamed of one . . . recently."

"You know, Mrs. Gibson, I've never had a real beau."

"That's surprising, Lucy."

"There's nobody in the Gap that interests me."

Dessie, looking into the cornflower blue eyes of the mayor's daughter, wondered how anyone so lovely could escape Cupid's arrows. "I'm sure you have plenty of suitors."

"Oh, yes. Unfortunately, I have boys following me around at every social Papa has. But I'm sick to death of shiftless boys in waistcoats and tails. Aren't there any *real* men left in the world, Mrs. Gibson?"

"I'm sure there's one for you somewhere!"

Lucy sighed. "I'd rather meet one that's a mite burly and savage than these spineless fish that run for their mother's petticoats at the first thing that displeases them!"

"How old are you, Lucy?"

"I just turned sixteen."

"You have plenty of time."

"That's what my mother says."

Deep and absorbing thoughts silenced Lucy for a while. Her delicate fingers folded and unfolded a piece of ribbon as she watched Dessie softly shirr the collar for the jade green dress she fashioned. "Mrs. Gibson?"

"Yes, Lucy. What's on your mind?"

"Did you have a beau when you were my age?"

Dessie looked up in surprise. "Why . . . yes, I did."

"What was he like? Was he . . . a real man or a boy?"

Dessie's eyes went beyond the windowpane, beyond the crab apple tree in the yard, and filled with a dreamy glow, lighted by memory's magic torch. "Oh, yes, he was a man all right. Square shoulders, ruddy face, clear mahogany eyes—like Mama used to say, he looked like a man you'd want to tie to and stick to till the war was over."

"Was he from your home town?"

"No, he wasn't. He came into my life quite suddenly from miles away."

"How long was it before you married him?"

"I didn't."

"But . . . why? Didn't you want to?"

"At the time I did. I would probably have married him on a wild impulse. But that wasn't the Creator's plan for me. Much later in life—six years later, in fact—I married Walter, a man I had known all my life, and I'll never regret it."

"Then it really wasn't love . . . the first one, I mean?"

"Oh, I wouldn't say that, Lucy. There's room in a human heart for more than one love in a lifetime if need be. And not all loves are alike. At sixteen, one's feelings can be very intense."

"What . . .because of that beau? Have you seen him since then?"

"I . . . don't know what path his life took. "I've only seen him once since then."

To thwart more questions, Dessie tactfully changed the subject. "Have you met the new school superintendent for our county, Lucy?"

Lucy folded her slender arms and took on a look of mild annoyance. "Yes, Mrs. Gibson, I have. Have you?"

"No."

"You'll meet him soon enough, I'm sure. I don't like the look in his eyes. It's . . . hard. I sure hope he doesn't give you a bad time."

"Your father talks like I won't have to cross roads with him very often."

"I hope not. He's good enough looking . . . and a real man, too. But something deep in his brown eyes gives me an uneasy feeling. Papa is glad he isn't local. It was rumored that he looked for property here, but couldn't find anything that pleased him."

"If he's so disagreeable, I'd say the farther away he lives, the better."

"That's my thinking. Here, Mrs. Gibson, let me do that hem-stitching for you. Mother says I make neat hems." Lucy bent her head of golden curls, bound with a blue ribbon that just matched her eyes, over the garment, her back to the front door, the light streaming over her shoulder.

The clatter of the treadle drowned out the whistle on Arthur's lips as he approached, his muscles taut against the weight of his portmanteau. Martha had sent no warning to Dessie that he was coming; she was not expecting him.

The bold knock on the door that could only have been administered by a powerful masculine hand brought Dessie abruptly to her feet. "Whoever could it be, Lucy?" she murmured, her expression puzzled.

It took a while for recognition and reality to meet. When they did, Dessie blinked, gasped, then wholly yielded to her sisterly joy. "Arthur! Whatever are you doing here?" She gave him a warm hug.

"Maw sent me to protect you." He grinned and Lucy turned about, catching the full impact of his handsome manliness.

"Lucy, this is my youngest brother, Arthur," Dessie introduced. "Isn't this a pleasant surprise? Arthur, this is Lucy, my neighbor."

Lucy nodded, seeing nothing but the handsome face, dark hair, brown eyes, and the blue homespun chambray shirt. Her face went white, and she arose to excuse herself. "I . . . must be going, Mrs. Gibson. I've already overstayed my time." And she was gone, fleeing as if she had seen a ghost.

Chapter Eight

Dinner with the Mayor

"Just you quit your worrying, Sister!" demanded Arthur. "There's some things we'll be needing, and I don't intend to sit here idle."

Against Dessie's tearful objections, Arthur went to work in the rock quarries, ignoring her phobia of falling rock. For a farm boy, accustomed to pay from the fall crops once a year, the weekly paycheck looked like a merchant's bankroll. Before the month was out, he purchased a one-horse shay to transport Dessie and Becky to and from the schoolhouse.

With Arthur around the place, life became less tedious. Three cherry blossom plates on the table lifted Dessie' flagging spirits, reminding her of happier days in the past. Arthur, jovial of nature, spread gaity like a communicable disease. Dessie found it hard to be depressed in his company.

Lucy's visits ceased. For some time, it did not dawn upon Dessie that Lucy equated the dream of the young man in the blue shirt with Arthur. She wondered at her absence, but said nothing.

"I met the mayor today," Arthur boasted one evening when Dessie dished up supper. "In fact, he invited me to his house for dinner. Why didn't you tell me you had such uptown friends, Sis?"

"That was the mayor's daughter you met the first day you came."

"The paragon of beauty that I frightened away?"

Dessie laughed. "They're our next door neighbors."

Arthur whistled. "Maybe I'd better start being more neighborly!"

"Arthur! What would Mama say if she heard you talking so foolishly? Besides, wasn't there a girl back home?"

"Out of sight, out of mind . . ." As a fortress against Dessie's scolding, he hurried on. "And being neighbors to the chief executive of this borough is all the more reason I need to clean up around this place. I start today." Slothfulness to Arthur represented sin. "Of what value is the old wheel leaning against the house? Sentimental? Wheel of fortune?"

"A friend borrowed it recently, and I was afraid he might need it again, so I left it there . . ."

"He?" Arthur raised his eyebrows quizzically.

"Arthur! Cut it out!" The tattling blush betrayed her.

"Why, Sis, there's nothing more romantic than loaning an old wagon wheel to a bachelor!"

"I didn't say he was single, Arthur. He probably has a wife and family. It was someone I had met years ago."

"Well, why didn't you *ask* after the welfare of his family and find out?"

"He didn't recognize me—and I wished it to stay that way. Incidentallly, he thought *I* was married. When he returned the wheel, he left a note of thanks for Walt."

"If he was just passing through, he probably won't be back to be needing the wheel."

"Probably not."

"But if you insist, of course, we'll leave the wheel there for good luck . . . each spoke a talisman . . ."

"Do whatever you wish with the wheel, Arthur. If it's an eyesore . . ."

"It's quite a conversation piece, really."

Arthur was not likely to remember either the arbor meeting or the preacher of ten years past. He had slept through every service until he was woefully too big for the pallet in the sawdust, giving little attention to the names of ministering evangelists or their offspring. This thought rested Dessie's mind.

The onset of school brought a welcome shortening of the onerous days Dessie had known since Walt's passing. Becky thrilled to the classroom atmosphere of studying children and adapted well. She soon became a beloved favorite of Dessie's pupils.

Dessie tried unsuccessfully to thrust from her mind the inevitable clash with the disagreeable county superintendent. Always modest and retiring, Dessie had no desire to be spotlighted in a city-county quibble.

So when Arthur came in saying that he had met the unpopular superintendent at the mayor's house, Dessie solicited his prognosis.

"How is it that you were at the mayor's house, anyhow?" she taunted, her sea-green eyes teasing.

"Don't you remember that I told you the mayor asked me to dinner?"

"I knew you put axle grease on your hair for some

reason!"

"To impress the mayor."

"You're very convincing, Arthur. And did you impress the mayor?"

Arthur grinned sheepishly. "I think so."

"Did he invite the superintendent, too? I thought Lucy told me her father and the new superintendent weren't exactly friends."

"No, the school officer showed up after our meal, to enquire of the mayor how the school system was running. He's taking his new job seriously."

"What is he like—this archenemy of mine whom I've never met?"

"You're not going to believe this, Sis. I like him a lot."

"Arthur, I don't suppose you've ever met a man you didn't like, have you?"

"Or a lady, either," smirked Arthur. "There's so much bad in the best of us and so much good in the worst of us, that I always say it all comes out even most of the time anyhow."

"What was he like?"

"He was two or three inches taller than I am, had black hair and brown eyes, and . . ."

"I didn't ask for a physical description, Arthur."

"Oh."

"What did he *act* like?"

"Oh, he was strictly business with the mayor. But then he asked me if I knew where any good fishing places were. And of course I said I did. You know me. Wherever I go, I learn all the fishing holes for a hundred miles around the first week I'm there."

"So?"

"He asked if he could go fishing with me sometime."

"What's his name?"

"He asked me just to call him Dave. I've forgotten his last name—if I ever heard it."

"You didn't tell him your sister was the teacher in the Gap, did you?"

"Of course not. It's more interesting to remain anonymous and see what happens."

"Lucy described him as having a . . . bad look in his eyes."

"You've got to learn what put it there before you can identify it, Sis. You women judge men too quickly . . . and too harshly."

"What age man is he?"

"That's the shocker. He's real young. He isn't much over thirty, or else he's mighty well preserved for his age. I don't know how he landed the job as superintendent."

"Nobody seems to know how he got it. And everybody wishes he hadn't."

"Is it a voted-in job or an appointed one, Dessie?"

"Appointed, I think."

"Then that would explain. Somebody in politics pulled some strings for him up front somewhere."

"I'm . . . dreading our inevitable meeting."

"No need dreading it, Sis. What is it Papa used to say? 'Don't go troublin' trouble til trouble troubles you,' or something like that."

"But I'm really the one on the wrong side of the fence, Arthur. Taking Becky to class is against the rules."

"I'll say Dave will be a stickler for rules. When it comes to the showdown, Dessie, it'll probably be your job or his. Because I don't think he'll bend."

63

"That's what I'm afraid of, Arthur. It's ridiculous. The school board could easily have chosen a teacher without a child and not have broken the rules."

"I really think the clash is between Dave and Mr. Wells . . . and sometimes I think it is purposeful."

"With me scissored in the middle."

"You think you're bad off, Sis. I'm the one who has the troubles."

"You?"

"Yours truly."

"How so?"

"Well, it's like this. The mayor likes me but he doesn't like the new superintendent. Dave likes me, but he doesn't like the mayor. I like Dave and I like the mayor. Lucy doesn't like the new superintendent, but I like Lucy. And I hope Lucy likes me."

Chapter Nine

A Fishing Trip

"*H*ave a good day, Sis." Arthur lifted Becky from the shay, rumpling her golden curls. "And mind the teacher, little lady."

Arriving at the schoolhouse an hour early so that Arthur could be on time at the quarry gave Dessie the leisure of prudently choosing the seeds of knowledge to be planted into the fertile minds of her pupils each day. Nor did she mind the afternoon wait. It gave her ample time for reflection and a chance to set her room in order.

Arthur looked back and waved. Some premonition told him that it was test day, not for the students, but for the teacher. And he winced at the thought. Dessie would have more than one strike against her.

He had not told Dessie about his fishing trip with Dave or what he had found out about the man. He thought back now to the Saturday past. Dessie supposed that he had gone for a ride with Lucy, and he made no effort to change her supposition. He felt much like a cornered chessman, moving precariously between friendships, jobs, Lucy, and his own sister.

He had met Dave at the stagecoach inn for a hurried breakfast, and the two had headed for the creek. Arthur was uncertain of the creek's name; the natives simply called it Clear Fork. To Arthur, names of waterways carried no importance as long as the fish were plentiful.

Dave followed him, morosely silent, to the low cliff overlooking a deeper part of the river. "Here's where we'll find them," Arthur promised.

Arthur flung himself into the spirit of fishing and had slipped a dozen fair-sized bass onto the stringer before he realized that Dave had tired of the sport and was staring across the stream into the mutiny of falling leaves and moss-robed rocks beyond.

Arthur, perceptive beyond his years and sensitive to the needs of others, knew that Dave needed a confidant. He lay down his pole, and when he turned toward his new friend, he saw a haunting look in the man's dark eyes that Lucy must have seen and misinterpreted as hardness.

"I thought it would help to get away," he apologized, meeting Arthur's gaze.

"Sometimes it does and sometimes it doesn't," Arthur replied wisely, neither pushing Dave to further conversation nor closing the door on more.

"Go ahead fishing, son. You're doing a good job. I wouldn't want to spoil a good fishing trip with my troubles."

"I've got about as many fish as I care to clean," Arthur smiled amiably. "Unless you want me to catch some more for you to take home with you."

"I don't have a home." The look combined bitterness

and hurt. "I live in a boarding house."

"I might be able to land enough for the whole boarding house."

"No, thanks. I've eaten greasy pork and greasy chicken and greasy mutton there—but I don't think I could stomach greasy fish." The man tried on a smile, but it fit poorly.

Slowly the story had tumbled out, often hanging on snags of bitter memory. "How old are you, Arthur?"

"Twenty."

"I was about your age when I married. She was a pretty little mite as girls go. I'd known her in upper school. We loved each other. A few of our differences were never resolved, but that's neither here nor there now. I got my higher education on the side after we married as I could and made a decent living for Earnestine . . ."

Dave paused, picking distractedly at a dried weed that had headed out to seed. Arthur listened, saying nothing.

"Happiness didn't come easy for me because of a truth I was once exposed to, but the day my baby girl was born was the day I walked on heaven's clouds. She came into the world bearing my resemblance and made my heart her captive. We both loved the baby—my wife and I—maybe too much."

A real pain filled Dave's eyes and tightened his facial muscles to a near grimace. Arthur's heart yearned to reach out and comfort him, but he sat motionless as Dave continued the heartbreaking story.

"She lived one year . . . the baby. One short, perfect year. It's as if I can remember every smile, every touch of her little hand. Then the second winter she took the croup. The doctor came. We hoped . . . and prayed. But she didn't make it."

Dave's words seemed to catch on a jagged stump.

"What was her name?" The question came out soft, gilded with sympathy.

"Tina—for Earnestine."

"There were . . . no more children?"

Dave's expression grew cold, a look that could have been mistaken for anger. "Earnestine never gave us the chance. She grieved herself to death for the child. I begged her to take nourishment, to put herself back together for my sake, promising her there would be more babies down life's road. But no! With Tina gone, she didn't want to live, she said. She wanted to go where Tina was. She didn't consider me, not caring that she left me alone in the world to fight my grief and loneliness single-handed! It would have been a pleasure to go myself. But one doesn't just will himself to die. At least a *man* doesn't. Earnestine did. It was *selfish* of her to die and leave me to suffer!"

Dave, almost shouting, caught himself and turned his head away to hide angry tears, jerking at the blades of brittle crab grass.

"How long ago has that been, Dave?" With emotions so fresh and cutting, Arthur supposed that the loss had been recent.

"Six long, lonely years of trying to forget! Six years of nightmares! Six years of sleepless nights and cold sweats and haunting memories!"

"I . . . understand." Of course, he didn't—couldn't.

"That's the reason I took this job with the school system. My father worried about my sanity and wanted to get me out of the country. An uncle of mine lived in this state and got me appointed at Father's request. I did need to get away. But I find that I am being followed. Followed by my past. Nothing will drown this terrible feeling. Not even a fishing trip."

"I'm . . . glad you told me."

"It was tell it or lose my mind. But I hate the boardinghouses. If I don't get out, I don't know what will happen. I start my rounds to the schools next week. I hope being busy with the new job will help."

"Have you ever considered marrying again and making a home?"

"I guess I don't trust women, Arthur. Another one might desert me. I can't conquer the feeling that Earnestine let me down. I've been looking around for other living arrangements, though. I've even considered buying property. There's a small place for sale on the outskirts of the Gap. I went to look it over last Sunday, but there was no one at home. I'm not even sure I was at the right location; I should get Mr. Davis to draw me a map. I might get you to go house hunting with me when I'm in the area."

"I'd be glad to."

"I've got to get out of that boardinghouse," Dave repeated doggedly.

A large-mouth bass jumped, his crystal scales mirroring the blue of the water. Arthur picked up his pole. "Let's see which one of us can get that beauty."

"As you say. The fish are all yours. Your mother can surely find room in the frying pan for one more fish."

Dave had never asked after Arthur's family, and Arthur volunteered no information. When he looked at Dave again, the haunting torment was hidden away, and his eyes held the challenge of man in contest with wildlife. The talk had been therapy for the bruised heart.

Chapter Ten

The Superintendent's Visit

"*L*ook, Mommy!"

With classes dismissed for the day and laughing, satchel-bearing children scattering in all directions, Dessie sat about to tidy up her disarrayed desk. She replaced the pen in the inkwell and dusted the erasers. A grammar assignment and several ungraded papers claimed her attention. She hummed a happy tune to match her light mood, her mental sky cloudless. Life had taken on purpose once again.

Lucy had stopped by her desk for a sisterly chat, asking about Arthur, when the bell clanged. Her eyes sparkled as she whispered into Dessie's ear. "Your brother is a real *man*, Mrs. Gibson. He likes to fish and hates dinner jackets. And would you believe, Papa even likes him!" Lucy skipped off, her musical laughter lingering.

At Becky's command, Dessie whirled about so quickly that the swirling skirt of her jade-colored dress scarcely had time to change directions with her, entangling her in its yardage. It was her favorite dress, bringing out the

71

flecks of amber in her green eyes.

Dessie looked . . . and then looked again, startled. Her face blanched from red to ashy white.

The tall man stood stiffly, adjusting his eyes to the building's shaded interior. "I'm sorry to be so late," he began. "I suppose the teacher has already left?"

"I'm the teacher," she said woodenly, supposing that he anticipated a spectacled spinster and mistook her for the mother of a student. "May I help you?"

"I'm the new county superintendent of schools and I . . ."

She gasped, she hoped imperceptibly.

His eyes adjusted to the room and fell upon Becky. Dessie watched him study the child's small face with a fatherly gentleness, but when Becky smiled up at him, the look turned to an unpredicted scowl, followed by a glare akin to hate.

"Is this your child, Mrs. . . ."

"Gibson is the name, sir."

". . . Gibson?"

"Yes, sir. This is Becky Gibson."

"You didn't bring her to class with you today, did you?"

"Yes, sir, I did."

"Did you not know that it is against policy for a teacher to bring a preschool child into the classroom? Many a mother would like to teach if we'd allow her to bring along all her offspring."

"I know the rules, sir."

"Then you have deliberately broken your teaching contract with the county, and that is ground for dismissal."

"I was careful to sign no such contract, sir."

"Excuse me. But are you the teacher heralded as having such outstanding credentials, hired by the mayor and approved by the entire school board of this city?"

"I hope so."

"You're not substituting?"

"No, sir."

"You have been here since the onset of school?"

"I have, sir."

"Did the honorable mayor not go over the rules in careful detail with you, Mrs. Gibson?"

"He did."

"Do you bring the child with you often, or is this a case of isolated emergency today?"

"I bring her every day."

"I'm sure the mayor is unaware of this."

"He is aware of it. You may ask him for yourself, sir."

"You can be sure that I will. You realize, I suppose, that I have the power to fire you on the spot."

"Yes, sir."

"Have you any plausible explanation to give for breaking the rules?"

"None other than what has already been discussed with the mayor and presented to the school trustees."

"Then I will give you one week to find a nursemaid for that child. There'll be no extension of time. If you do not comply readily and willingly, you will find yourself without a job. There will be no tolerance. Do you understand?"

"Quite well, sir."

"I . . ." The superintendent stopped abruptly and studied Dessie's face. She lowered her eyes, fearing that time would betray her and and roll back as it had once done. "You're the woman I borrowed the wheel from, aren't you?"

"Yes, sir. I remember you coming by."

"Did you find the note I left for your husband?"

"Yes, sir."

"The mayor tells me you are indeed an exceptional teacher. We'd hate to lose you." His voice softened. "But my job is to see that rules are strictly kept. I'll be checking back next week."

Dessie stared at the place where he stood long after he was gone. She still shook with rigorous intensity when Arthur came for her. Her lips quivered and her hands trembled.

Arthur surmised right away what had happened; Dave had told him he would make the rounds this week. The day of reckoning had unnerved Dessie.

"Why, Sis, what's wrong?" he asked solicitously.

"The . . . superintendent came by just now."

"It couldn't have been that bad. You look like you've seen a ghost."

"It . . . was . . . bad." Dessie's pent up emotions gave way to tears.

"What did he say, Dessie? He's my friend and I'll see what I can do . . ."

"Arthur, please stay out of this. Whatever you do, don't let him find out that you even know me."

"Did he give you your walking papers, Sis?"

"Not yet. But he plans to."

"When?"

"Next week."

"Don't worry about it, Dessie. It isn't that important.

I'll take care of you and Becky. I have a good job. That's
what Paw sent me here for."

Dessie sobbed brokenly. "That's sweet of you, Arthur.
I did so enjoy teaching, though. It shortened the hours
and took my mind off . . . all that has happened."

"I'm sorry the superintendent gave you a hard time."

"I . . . can't stand the way he looked . . . at Becky."
More tears flowed.

Arthur put his arm about his sister. "Tell me about
it."

"When he first saw her, he looked so . . . so tender-
ly at her. Then the look turned to . . . to hate or something. It almost frightened me." Dessie buried her face
in her hands.

"Dessie, could I ask one thing of you?"

"Y-yes. What?"

"Don't judge the man too harshly. He's had a hard
life. He's . . . he's got a good heart down underneath it
all."

"I . . . I think I'll just quit."

"No, Dessie, you mustn't. It's not what God would
want you to do. That's the coward's way. There's a lot
of rough edges that's got to be knocked off all of us—me
and Dave and the mayor—and you are a key figure in
God's work. Hang in and let Dave fire you . . . if he can."

"Dave?"

"That's the superintendent's first name. Remember,
I told you . . ."

"Dave who?"

"I don't know his last name."

"Is it Dave Parsons?"

"That's it! Parsons!"

It's Nathan Parsons, Arthur. Dessie wanted to say it, but Arthur would wonder how she knew. No, there could never be a duplicate of those wine-brown eyes, the wavy hair, the furrowed chin.

Nathan Parsons. A School Superintendent? Arthur said he'd had a hard life. What could have put that hardness in his eyes? And what was he trying to run from by changing his name from Nathan to Dave?

So she had one more week to teach school. Each of her students had become dear to her. Mayor Wells vowed he'd win in the city-county confrontation, but after today's encounter with Nathan Parsons, Dessie had her doubts.

Chapter Eleven

Overheard Plans

Men scuttled this way and that, carrying battered pails. It was lunch time at the quarries.

Behind a massive rock with a flat, smooth top overlooking the gaping hole into which seeped a few inches of lime water, Arthur spread the repast that Dessie had packed for him. Not normally a loner, he now sought a place of solitude to think over a solution for Dessie. She loved teaching school, and he wished to see her happy.

And now she had one short week before her job would be terminated—or at least suspended until the city and county could resolve their differences. Dave would fight for principles, and Mr. Wells would fight for practicality in spite of rules. It promised to be a bitter battle.

The cake and dried fruit Dessie had put into his lunchbox added life to the otherwise sterile meal. She tucked in little surprises every day. That was so much like Dessie, supplementing a bleak daily existence with small gems of pleasure. Her teaching was the same way; that's why her pupils loved her and learned more than book knowledge. If only Dave knew . . .

"What I need is a woman to pack my dinner fer me."
The coarse, careless talk floated down from the pinnacle
of the rock above. Arthur couldn't help but hear.

"Another woman is jest what you don't need, Slats,"
contradicted another crude male voice. "You left a good
'un with two bright younguns to feed back in Aspermont.
Many a man'd consider hisself lucky to have a woman like
Beatrice."

"Got bored with that 'un."

"'Cause she didn't dance to yore tune. You'd get
bored with another'n."

"Naw, I wouldn't. I've found out batchin's no fun
atall."

"Go back to Beatrice and the kids."

"Not on yore life! She's a fergotten item as fer as I'm
concerned."

Arthur recognized the voices of two brothers the
straw boss called Slats and Dink Cunningham. He picked
up his lunch bucket to move to another location so as not
to be an unwitting eavesdropper, but the next part of their
conversation stopped him dead in his tracks.

"You don't got one spotted, have ye, Slats?"

"Yep, I have. You know th' young widder woman o'
Walt Gibson . . ."

"Th' man that was killed by th' fallin' rock here at
th' quarries a year er so back?"

"That 'un."

"I remember awright. Shook up th' whole town."

"Left a right fetchin' wife behind."

"You see 'er?"

"Seen 'er goin' in Mr. Davis's office one day last sum-

78

mer. She held 'er head high an' stepped proud-like. A sporty one. Couldn't speak to 'er cause 'er old man was visitin' from somewhere down state. So I jest leaned meself agin a buildin' an' watched. Th' sun shimmered 'er hair, makin' it goldish, an' th' best I could see, she had git-an-bring-um-back eyes."

"How do you know she'd give you th' time o' day, Slats? Yore right conceited . . .''

Slats guffawed, a sound that grated Arthur's nerves. "Have you ever seen a woman I couldn't snow, Dink? Now have ye?"

"Has she got kids?"

"Heard say she has one little sobber, a'ready dry an' out o' rompers."

"You ain't proved very handy with kids, Slats. Don't think enough o' th' two you got to send 'em a piece o' bread."

"She won't have to know that, Dink. I can put on an act that'll beat vaudeville." Another raucous laugh sliced the humid air.

"She got 'er own property?"

"'Deed she does—a nice bit—an' I'd shore like to get my hands on it. It's over by th' mayor's place. I hear she's got a job ateachin' school, too. A money-makin' woman's jest what I need."

"What you need is some sense in yore head."

Slats ignored Dink's caustic remark. "See, I could let 'er support me fer a while. I'm plum' tired o' workin' here in these quarries. I'm hankerin' to loaf awhile."

"Ifn I know you, Slats, you stay tired o' workin'. Why, I remember when you was still in knee britches, you'd cut all kinds o' didoes to get outta work. An' you hain't never changed."

"Jest my nature, I guess."

"Paw oughtta thrashed that nature outta ya."

"Paw couldn't ketch me. He was too drunk most o' th' time."

"When you goin' to see this fetchin' lady?"

"Oh, I'm bidin' my time. I'll know when th' apple's ripe. Then I'll move in fer th' pickin'."

"Don't she have a brother that works out here?"

"Yeah. Name o' Arthur Harris. But he's th' pious kind—won't give nobody no trouble. In-laws don't cramp my style none nohow."

"Ifn you don't git a move on, somebody may beat you to th' draw. Ifn she's all that pleasin', other eyes may be watchin' 'er."

"I'm keepin' tabs, Dink. She ain't sparked no one since th' accident."

"What ifn she finds out 'bout Beatrice an' th' kids back in Aspermont?"

"How could she? Nobody here knows my back life but you, an' ifn she learns 'bout it, I'll know 'twas you what squealed an' it'll be yore skin to pay, I promise you."

"It looks suspicious-like fer a man as old as you to be unhitched, Slats."

"I'll make up some convincin' Job story 'bout losin' my kith an' kin. Ladies er easy criers, an' when they get to feelin' sorry fer ye, you can swing th' sundial yore way ever' time."

Arthur's skin prickled, first cold and then hot. Why, these uncouth men were talking about his own sister! Waves of anger rolled over his irate soul, washing up a debris of bad feelings. He wanted to walk up to the offender and punch his nose, but of course, that would defeat his purpose. The scoundrel must not know that his plans had been heard, thereby allowing Arthur the time and freedom to outmaneuver him. Forewarned was forearmed, Papa always said. When the waves of anger went back to sea and left the shore of his mind clear again, he thanked God for allowing him to overhear Slat's plans, and he took the news straight home to Dessie.

"Sis, I have something I need to tell you . . ."

"You aren't leaving, are you, Arthur?" A worry crossed Dessie's brow.

"No."

"Or getting married?"

"No. What I need to tell you concerns *you,* not me."

"More troubles?"

"There's a man planning on calling on you . . ."

Dessie almost dropped the age-browned ironstone bowl of gravy she held in her hands. "A man . . . calling on me?"

"Yes. And with the intention of proposing marriage."

"You must be mistaken, Arthur. I'm not that well acquainted with any gentleman . . ."

"No, I'm not mistaken."

"How . . . did you find out?"

"I found out today by accident. I'd . . . rather not discuss it yet, so don't ask me any questions. Just trust me. The man has a shady past and would not be good for you . . . or Becky, either. He's a married man with two children, trying to cover his past."

"When is he coming?"

"I don't know. He's biding his time, though. But, Sis, if a man comes—any man—don't fall for his line. He'll be

81

lying to you."

Dessie shuddered. "Oh, Arthur. I . . . don't feel safe."

"You're safe enough and have nothing to worry about with me around. I just thank God that Papa sent me to look after you. I shun the thought of what might happen if I wasn't around."

"But I don't understand, Arthur. Why would he call on me?"

"You're . . . pretty. He knows you have a job . . . and property. He wants your property."

"Oh, Arthur . . ."

"Now don't be frightened, Sis. He won't pull any funny stuff all at once. His methods will be slow, but determined, I'm afraid."

Chapter Twelve

Unwanted Visitor

"*L*ooks like we're in for rain." Arthur bridled the horse to a stop at the schoolhouse door and helped Dessie and Becky from the surrey.

Black clouds boiled restlessly overhead, sending a few bold drops of rain vying for first place in the race toward earth, braving the way for others.

Dessie sniffed the air. "Smells like rain, too. Do you suppose it will rain you out of work?"

"That's possible. But a few days of rest won't hurt me any. I have a little money put back for a rainy day."

By noon, the weather had shut the quarries down, and Arthur returned home. Staving off idleness, he wrote Martha and Henry a hurried letter with sentences so abbreviated that the missive needed but a few "stops" here and there and a yellow hue to transform it to a telegram. He shared only the good news, telling them he had a good job, but purposely failed to mention where. Martha would be sure to worry—or even call him home—if she knew he worked in the mines where Walt had lost his life. He placed Dessie's Brazos Point address on the back of the envelope, then slept until time to pick her up.

Although she was free to leave at the the toll of the dismissal bell, Dessie insisted on staying the extra hour that she had become accustomed to. On this day Arthur arrived early, smitten by cabin fever and hoping to see Lucy. He offered to drive her home while Dessie lingered to set her classroom in order.

Lucy turned her beautiful sky-blue eyes upon him soberly. "Mrs. Gibson seems troubled today, Arthur. What is bothering her?"

"Didn't you know about the county superintendent coming last week?"

"No, I didn't see him."

"It must have been after the classes dismissed."

"Was he rude to her, Arthur?"

"Not rude, exactly. He was unhappy when he learned that she had brought Becky with her to classes."

"Becky doesn't bother anybody."

"But rules are rules."

"Papa expected he'd be displeased. But she's still teaching . . ."

"This is her last week . . . unless she finds a nursemaid for Becky."

"She'll never do that."

"No, she won't. As much as she loves teaching, she loves Becky more."

"I don't blame her. No job is worth leaving your baby for."

"Not if there's any other way. And since I'm working, there's another way."

"Papa won't let Dave Parsons fire Mrs. Gibson." Lucy

squared her shoulders and looked defiantly at Arthur through those azure eyes. "She's the best teacher the Gap has ever had. Papa says she can teach better holding to a child with one hand than most teachers can teach using both hands—and that's true."

"She . . . loves her pupils. I . . . hope your father will have some influence . . ."

He took Lucy's small hand and helped her to the ground, holding it longer than necessary. She smiled coyly, blinking her long, smoky lashes and sending the memory of her loveliness with him.

"Surely the superintendent won't come checking up on me in this rain, will he, Arthur?" Dessie asked the hopeful question before they reached the bridge.

"Rain won't stop Dave, Dessie. If he said he'd be back this week, he will be back. Rain or shine."

Dessie sighed. "I just got Jacob Millet to where he'd recite for me. The next teacher will have to start all over. And little Annie Rushing needs a second reader already . . . and I'll miss Lucy so dreadfully!"

Arthur sat in pensive silence. At last he spoke. "Eventually the showdown will come, Dessie, but I've thought of a way we might stall it off."

"How's that, Arthur?"

"As long as it's raining and I can't work, I can keep Becky at home with me. I can bring her to see you at lunch time if you wish. If Dave comes and she's not there, he'll assume that you have complied with the rules."

"Wouldn't that be deceit?"

"Not unless you're untruthful. He probably won't ask any questions. The conclusions he draws will be those of his own making."

85

"That would give me a few more days . . ."

"Or even weeks."

"And I do hate to leave unfinished tasks."

With Becky to care for, Arthur forfeited his early afternoon arrivals at the school to visit Lucy, often slipping off to see her in the evenings instead. But in spite of his jokes about enjoying the rest, he found himself growing fidgety with too much time on his hands granted him by the inclement weather. He longed to be occupied again.

One afternoon, a heavy knock on the door sent Becky racing to see who was there. "Howdy, little lady," a raspy male voice just beyond the reach of Arthur's recognition said. "Is yore mammy at home?"

"No," Becky said simply, running back toward Arthur timidly.

Arthur, face-to-face with the well-dressed suitor, combed his memory to place the man. It took him a few seconds to identify Slats Cunningham, transformed in a handsome coat and top hat, presenting an impressive image. Arthur had never envisioned Slats as good-looking, but with his thick auburn hair well groomed, his mustache waxed, and his beard smartly trimmed, he could hardly be recognized as the unrefined quarry worker who had raised Arthur's ire.

"Th' young lady there tells me 'er maw ain't home."

"No, she isn't." Arthur meant for Slats to feel the chill of his words.

But Slats wasn't to be deterred so easily. "Will she be comin' in presently? I could jest wait fer 'er."

"Will you be so kind as to state your business here?" Arthur knew Slat's business but masked his knowledge well with the icy question.

"I've come to see th' lady."

"About what?"

"About marryin' me."

"My sister will not marry you."

"I think 'twould be best ifn you let yore sister speak fer 'erself."

"No, it wouldn't. I am here to protect my sister against just such characters as yourself."

"Don't jedge me afore you know me."

"I probably know a heap more about you that you'd like me to know," Arthur said frostily.

Slats looked abashed. "You must have me mixed up with somebody else, Mister. I'm Slatson J. Cunningham."

"That's who I was afraid you were, though I hardly recognized you in sheep's clothing."

"I'm here in yore town on a work assignment y'know. I have oil interests out in th' West."

"If that's the truth, that's not all you have out West."

Slats ignored the interruption and hurried on. "Somebody referred yore sister to me as a good prospect fer a wife since she was widdered last year an' lonely an' all. I even heared that she had a fetchin' little mite that'd steal any man's heart right outta 'is body—an' shore 'nough, there she is." He smiled superficially at Becky, who backed away distrustfully.

"My sister is a Christian and has very high principles."

"Oh, so I hear. That's th' kind I'm innerested in, bein' an upright kind o' man meself . . ."

". . . and therefore wouldn't even keep company with a man who has already deserted a wife and two children."

87

Slats hid his shock, but not quite soon enough. "I don't know where you heared those awful lies, Mister, less'n 'twas my scoundrel brother that's been talkin' falsehoods to you at th' quarries."

"I haven't talked to your brother."

Relief showed on Slat's features. "I once was married, sir." An actor he was and a deceiver, projecting a dog-eyed sadness.

"And still are."

"No, sir, you are mistaken. The girl I married met 'er death in a house fire, along with my new babe. I cried fer two whole years. I . . . I can scarce talk o' it yet without tears. It strikes so close to my achin' heart . . ." Pools of water actually clouded Slats' eyes.

"I'd like to strike close to your *nose!*" Arthur spat angrily. "I've a mind to write Beatrice Cunningham in Aspermont and tell her exactly where you are! You no-account rascal, leaving her with those two precious children. You don't deserve the breath God gives you to breathe this minute. Only a selfish brute would do something like that. The Bible says a man that won't take care of his own family is worse than an infidel. I'd be ashamed to be called a man if I was you! You're not a man; you're a spineless sissy! Get off this property before I do something I wish I hadn't!" Arthur hadn't meant to say so much.

Slats backed away from the door hurriedly, seeking escape. "I . . . I . . ."

"Don't ever set foot on this place again, Slats Cunningham! You tempt my Christian temperance."

In the race for a safe exit, Slats lost his silk top hat. He glanced about nervously, as if trying to decide whether retrieving it was worth the risk, then dashed back for it, and scurried out the gate. Arthur watched his fleeing form and would have laughed had he not been so angry.

Slowly his fists unclenched. "Let's go get Dessie, Becky," he said abruptly. "But we won't say a word to her about the rapscallion that came."

"Who?"

"Never mind."

Chapter Thirteen

Bridge Washout!

"I've always wondered what the purpose of this old wooden bridge was," Arthur commented when he took Dessie to school that morning. "Now I know."

Dessie looked down into the churning water that slapped against the bridge supports with hostile intent. The rains filled the dry gulch between her property and the schoolhouse, necessitating a means of crossing.

"Keep Becky in at noon, Arthur. No need bringing her out to share lunch with me in this mess. This is Friday and I can stand one day without seeing her. I won't worry; I know she's in good hands."

"And I've got a feeling the superintendent might show up today, Dessie."

"A cheerful thought!"

By midday, Dessie was glad that she had insisted on Arthur keeping Becky in the warm and dry house. The whipping torrents beat crazily against the windowpanes, distracting the children from their studies, and the wind took on a biting chill. Jagged lightning and rumbling thunder set her nerves on edge, making her jumpy. Nathan Parsons would have to be out of his wits to come on a day like this!

Near two o'clock, a dripping figure wreathed in a rain slicker appeared in the doorway. Water ran from the deep wave in the front of his hair and dripped off the end of his nose. He turned his searching eyes from desk to desk, then fastened them on Dessie, apparently satisfied with what he saw . . . or didn't see.

"Mrs. Gibson," his voice carried the authority of his position. "The rain has let up temporarily. I'm asking that you dismiss school and send the children to their homes. It looks like there may be more rain coming, and the creek is rising fast."

"Yes, sir." Dessie motioned for an older boy to ring the bell. "Put your books away, students. You are dismissed. I'll see you Monday."

"And you may go, too," Nathan Parsons nodded toward Dessie.

"I have to wait for my ride."

"Which way is your place?"

Dessie's throat constricted, and her heart rate increased perceptibly. Surely, Nathan Parsons wasn't going to offer her a ride! Her cheeks flushed hotly. "North of here."

"Across the arroyo?"

"Yes, sir."

"Then I hope your husband comes early today. The stream will not be crossable much longer."

He disappeared, leaving a puddle of water where he had stood. A strange emptiness, greater than that of the empty building about her, swallowed Dessie. The pupils had gone home, Becky was safe with Arthur and . . . Nathan Parsons had left, thinking her married! What had she wanted him to do? Stay with her until Arthur came for her? It was likely that he was married. She lay her head on her desk, an overwhelming desire to cry gripping her.

She had seen the triumph in Nathan's eyes when he saw that Becky was absent. He thought she had complied with his rules. But it was she who had won a victory. Temporarily, anyhow. Her job would probably not be threatened for a few more days. Yet the victory held no sweetness.

"Your mother may get worried about you, Becky-girl," Arthur told the child, speaking to her as he would another adult, his equal. "The rising wash could cut us off if we don't get across. We'd best go early."

The child focused her wise, round eyes on him with trust and nodded. "Yes, we'd best."

Arthur reached the bridge and headed south for the school as Nathan Parsons made his way northward again. The turbulent waters pulled at the moorings and shook the frail structure that stretched from bank to bank.

"Where are you going?" yelled Nathan above the den of the rushing current.

"I'm taking the child to her mother." Arthur pointed to Becky sitting beside him in the buggy. Nathan did not know that Dessie was his sister, and Dessie had sworn him to secrecy.

A loud crack struck terror to Nathan's heart. "Get off the bridge, Arthur!" he screamed frantically. "It's giving way!"

But it was too late. With a dizzy swirl, the supporting timber turned loose, throwing the light shay into the air like a twig. Becky fell out of the conveyance and into the raging river.

In an instant, Nathan had flung himself into the tossing flood waters in an effort to save her. Stroke over stroke, he willed his powerful muscles to reach the struggling child, who bobbed up and down in the foaming tumult, bravely trying to keep her head up.

"Stay in there, kiddo," he shouted his encouragement. "Keep that head up!" She could not possibly have heard him.

With a backward glance, Nathan caught a nightmarish glimpse of Arthur's horse clawing for higher ground, dragging the crippled shay along. Arthur had apparently been struck by a bridge beam or other floating debris. Above the rolling waves, Nathan saw Lucy running to the river's edge in an attempt to minister to Arthur's needs.

In one brief instant when a thousand thoughts can flash through the mind with lightning speed, Nathan wondered where Lucy came from; he had not seen her as he crossed the bridge. He thanked God that Arthur was on the "home" side of the flood waters. Lucy would take care of him; he must concentrate on saving the girl that Arthur was taking to her mother. Unless he was mistaken, this was the teacher's child. Why did Arthur feel he must take the child to her mother in this wretched weather? Why couldn't the child's father or the new nursemaid have cared for her at home until the teacher returned? Or could it be that Arthur's mother *was* the child's nurse and she had solicited Arthur's help in getting the child to her mother at the close of school? The present peril gave Nathan no lesiure to sort through the file of possibilities for an answer.

In spite of Nathan's keen ability as a swimmer and his unusual physical strength, Becky tumbled down the deadly stream just out of his reach. He sent up a frantic prayer when it seemed she would surely be drowned. At last she latched onto a tree limb within her reach and clung to it for her life. *She's a fighter, that little one,* he said to himself. *From spunky stock, no doubt.* He wished he had shed his rain slicker before he plunged in, but it was too late to think of that now. He struggled on.

When at length he reached her, he found that she neither whimpered nor cried as most children her age would have done. She locked her arms about his neck in a grip that amazed him. "You're not much bigger than a wharf rat," he muttered, "and just as wet."

He tried to swim for shore, but as the river pushed southeast it widened, and his strength was no match for the heavy current. Now he feared that they might both be destroyed.

He prayed again, as his mother had taught him to do in early childhood. "It doesn't matter about me, God. I haven't been a very good Christian," he heard himself imploring. "I surely don't deserve to ask favors, but the teacher seems awfully fond of this child. I suppose it's the only one she and her husband have. Please let me save the child's life for the teacher's sake." In his mind, he saw the sea-green eyes of the teacher with their brownish-gold flecks. They reminded him of someone he had met long ago—someone who now hid in the far corners of his memory, refusing to step out into the light. The dim memory was pleasant at this moment when death seemed imminent.

When all hope seemed gone, the current pushed him up onto a small bar where the waters split and then joined again. The island scarcely large enough for the two occupants, stood a mere six inches above the water level. Should the waters rise more, they would again be washed away.

Nathan looked toward the tempestuous sky. It was clearing. The rain had stopped.

Chapter Fourteen

A Seeking Student

"*T*eacher's still at the schoolhouse, Papa," young Melissa Whitt told her father, a member of the Gap's school board. "If the bridge is out, she can't get home."

"We'd best go see about her, Melissa," Mr. Whitt said.

They found Dessie with her head on her arms, asleep.

"You'll have to come home with us, Mrs. Gibson. The river got up and washed the bridge away, and they'll have to wait until the water goes down a mite before they repair it. Shouldn't be too long, though, unless it sets in to raining again."

"The bridge?"

"Over Dry Gulch."

"What time did it wash out, Mr. Whitt?" asked Dessie, anxiously.

"Nobody saw it go. It was gone at three o'clock. I think all the youngsters who needed to cross had gotten across safely, so it must have broken up somewhere between two and three this afternoon. The mayor'll get a repair crew out there as soon as possible."

Dessie calculated that Arthur would not be at the crossing at that time of day as he never picked her up before half past four. He had found that the bridge was out, she reasoned, and returned home knowing that she would be safe in the home of one of her students on the opposite side of the river and would not be worried about him and Becky at home.

"I'm glad Mr. Parsons came and dismissed classes early so that everyone could get home safely," she said.

The five members of the Whitt family entertained her graciously, but throughout the evening, Dessie fought back prickles of warning that crept into her mind. She pushed the concern back as pointless.

When Mrs. Whitt showed her to the guest room, Melissa followed her shyly. "Now, Melissa," Mrs. Whitt cautioned in a motherly tone, "you must not bother Mrs. Gibson . . ."

"Oh, she's no bother, Mrs. Whitt," responded Dessie quickly. "Let her stay and visit with me awhile. Her company will help me pass the time and keep me from being so lonesome for Becky. I'm not sure that I can go to sleep away from her anyhow."

Melissa's quiet depth and sensitive spirit reminded Dessie of her own fourteenth year, when childhood was pulling her back and adulthood was pushing her forward. She recalled the tearing-apart feeling that was remedied only by the blessed passage of time.

Dessie sat in the cushioned rocker, and Melissa pulled up the crewelwork footstool nearby. The kerosene lamp's dancing flame cast playful shadows over the shiplap wall.

"Mrs. Gibson." Melissa wasted no time getting to the point, goaded on by an inner hunger. "I've been wanting to talk to you for a long time. I prayed for a chance, but I didn't know it would take a flood! You are such a good person; you must be a Christian."

"*Christian* is a pretty general term nowadays, Melissa, but I've been saved since I was fifteen years old. I don't know what I would have done without the Spirit of God within me."

"I *want* to be a Christian, Mrs. Gibson. How do you get to be one?"

"You have to be born one, dear."

"Oh, I see. I guess that lets me out. I'm . . . I'm sure I wasn't born one."

"But you can be."

"Now I've already been born, though. I can't be born over again."

"But you can, dear. You remind me of a man in the Bible named Nicodemus."

"I do? How?"

"Do you have a Bible?"

"There's one on the mantle. It belonged to my grandmother. I'll fetch it."

Melissa tiptoed out for the Bible, leaving a crack in the door to give her light and feeling her way along cautiously so as not to disturb the rest of the family, who had retired for the night.

Dessie turned to the third chapter of the Gospel of John. "This man, Nicodemus, thought the same thoughts you are thinking. 'How can a man be born when he is old?' he asked Jesus. But Jesus explained that He was talking about a *spiritual* birth. He said, 'Except a man be born of water and of the Spirit, he cannot enter into the kingdom of God. That which is born of the flesh is flesh; and that which is born of the Spirit is spirit. Marvel not that I said unto thee, Ye must be born again.' See, it's here in verses five, six, and seven."

"Yes, I see."

"But, of course, when Jesus was talking to that man, He hadn't died on the cross yet. He had to go to Calvary to die for our sins so that we could receive the new birth. A born-again Christian has been cleansed by the blood of Jesus so that he can live a new life."

"Please tell me more, Mrs. Gibson."

"The Gospels tell us the story of the life of Jesus. He spent three and a half years schooling His disciples to teach the world His plan for being born into His kingdom."

Melissa moved the stool closer, listening raptly. "Go on. What was His plan?"

"The Book of Acts gives us the pattern. Chapter two records how that Christ started His church on the Day of Pentecost. He poured out the Spirit that He had promised to the world, and then Peter preached the first sermon of the New Testament church. Peter proclaimed the simple gospel message of the death, burial, and resurrection of Jesus Christ. Those who heard it realized that they were sinners and asked, 'What shall we do?' And Peter, the disciple to whom Jesus had given the keys of the kingdom of heaven, told them."

"What did he tell them?"

"Here it is in verse 38: 'Repent, and be baptized every one of you in the name of Jesus Christ for the remission of sins, and ye shall receive the gift of the Holy Ghost.'

That's how we respond to the gospel, Melissa. Repentance is death to sin, baptism is burial with Jesus Christ, and the Holy Ghost gives new life and resurrection power. This Acts 2:38 experience is the new birth.''

"What is the gift of the Holy Ghost like? How will I know when I have received this gift?''

Dessie smiled at the endless barrage of questions from the child standing on the periphery of adulthood. "You'll know! You'll receive the gift just like they did in the Bible. The Holy Spirit is still the same! Look at verse four of chapter two: 'And they were all filled with the Holy Ghost, and began to speak with other tongues, as the Spirit gave them utterance.' When you're born into this brand-new kingdom, you'll speak a brand-new language.''

"But I'm afraid I can't speak any other language.''

"By yourself, you can't. But when you are born again, the Spirit gives you the 'utterance,' or the words to say.''

"Did you speak in a new language, Mrs. Gibson?''

"Indeed, I did! I've never felt more wonderful than I did at the moment when I knew I was born again as God's child and adopted into His spiritual family.''

"Is it for everybody?''

"Peter said, 'The promise is unto you, and to your children, and to all that are afar off.' I'd say that includes you and me. At first people thought this experience was only for the Jews, but in the tenth chapter of Acts, the Bible says, 'On the Gentiles also was poured out the gift of the Holy Ghost.' And everyone knew when it happened, 'for they heard them speak with tongues.' ''

Engrossed in leading a seeking soul to the Savior, Dessie passed the time joyfully. Papa always said that every cloud had a silver lining.

101

When at last she lay her head on the strange bolster, content that God had sent her into Melissa's home, and prayed for her child's protection, she could never have guessed that Nathan Parsons held Becky in his arms through that long, dark night.

Chapter Fifteen

A Miserable Night

"*L*ooks like we've landed on the isle of Melita, little one," Nathan mused, casting his eyes about, for he had heard his father preach many sermons on the life of Apostle Paul. "Now if we can just stave off the cold and the snakes."

Becky looked at him quizzically, a faint trace of a smile playing at the corners of her mouth.

"What's your name?" he asked her.

"Becky Ann Gibson."

"Hmmm. You can talk."

"Yes, I can talk." Her look accused him of being the immature one, and he laughed. "What's *your* name?"

"My name is Nathan." He said it before he thought, but then a child this young probably would not remember a name anyhow.

"That's a pretty name."

"Well, Becky Ann, this will probably be our Ararat until the waters go down. But that shouldn't take too many hours."

"My mother calls me just Becky."

"Is your mother the schoolteacher?"

"Yes."

The wet ringlets plastered to her small head, the lips blue with cold, and the fingers wrinkled from being in the water too long dug trenches in Nathan's fatherly heart. Her smallness almost frightened him. Six years had erased the memory of a child's diminutive size. He would have to think of some way to keep her warm, or she would die of exposure after he had saved her from a death of drowning.

He was glad now for the waterproof slicker, though it had done him no good during his swim. It would be a shield for Becky against the cold of the night.

As an early evening blackness meshed with the dark waters, he wrapped her in the cloak and held her close to himself to give her warmth. He knew she must be chilled and hungry, but not once did she complain. He had never seen a braver child.

A rodent tried to invade their island sometime during the endless night. Nathan kicked at it, trying not to awaken Becky. He dared not sleep lest the water rise or a venomous snake wash upon the tiny knoll.

The miserable night took on eternal proportions, giving Nathan time for serious soul-searching. He admitted to his nagging conscience that he had come to this part of the country seeking to escape from himself. He had adopted the use of his middle name, David, shortened it to Dave, and left his native state in an effort to lose his identity and to flee the truth he knew he must someday face. He had considered exposing his inner turmoil to Arthur Harris—the boy seemed level-headed and mature for his years. Now Arthur might be dead.

Before morning, Nathan sensed a tightening in his chest. The time spent in the icy, muscle-cramping waters together with the frigid wind that now tore through his damp clothing were taking their toll on him. He shivered.

Becky stirred at daylight and opened her eyes. They were sunken with hunger and fatigue. "I'm thirsty," she whispered. He hesitated to allow her to drink the river water, but he had no choice. He remembered Earnestine saying that a child could dehydrate fast. He made a cup of his big palm and filled it with water for Becky to drink from, praying that the dirty water would not make her ill.

"Thank you," she said.

It's up to me to save this child's life, he told himself, *and the battle is far from won.* The only logical thing to do was to try to swim with her to the "home" shore and get her back to her mother. If he waited longer, he would only grow weaker himself. Already, he could feel his strength waning. The waters were abating and looked less formidable than they did yesterday, for which he was thankful.

"We've got to get to shore, Becky," he told her. "Your mother will be worrying herself sick over you."

"She's at school."

"This being Saturday, she'll be at . . ." He stopped, considering that she was probably cut off from her home by the rampant tide, stranded at the schoolhouse or at the home of a friend. ". . . I don't know where she'll be," he finished lamely, not wishing to disturb the little girl. Mrs. Gibson had been waiting for her husband when he had left the school.

Weakness gnawed away at his strength, but he

blamed it on the lack of food and sleep. He feared waiting any longer to cross the stream, considering time his bitter enemy. So with Becky once more clinging to his neck, he thrust himself into the mad rush of water again, leaving behind the cumbersome raincoat, and struggled doggedly against the powerful force that opposed him. He found himself being pushed farther downstream.

Panic clawed at his mind. He should have never left the safety zone. Then he had an idea. Focusing his attention solely on a large tree on the shore, he swam for it, letting nothing divert his mind. Breathing heavily, he flung himself onto the bank at the foot of the tree, too tired to stand up. He and Becky were safe.

The sun emerged from its week-long hiding and peeped over the horizon. Nathan judged it must be about six o'clock.

Shaking with a feverish chill, Nathan arose and took Becky by the hand. "Can you walk?"

"Yes, I can walk."

"It's a mile to town."

"Is that far?"

"I never thought of it as being far . . . but today it's a mighty long way." A clammy sweat beaded Nathan's forehead.

Becky said nothing on the march, stumbling now and then on a stone, but bravely forging on. Her stamina astonished Nathan. He found himself wondering if his Tina would have been this courageous in the face of such adversity.

Near the general store, Nathan spotted the night watchman completing his beat. "Sir!" he called out, and the man turned around. "I'm Na . . . uh, Dave Parsons, the county school superintendent. This child belongs to the teacher here at the Gap. She was separated from her mother by the high flood waters. If you will take her to the mayor, he'll see that she gets home. And I'll see that you are properly paid." He placed Becky's small hand in the hand of the officer, then staggered off, hoping to reach his boardinghouse room before he grew too faint to walk. To fall by the way could mean death for him; no one knew where he was or would bother to come looking for him.

"Humph!" the sullen night patrol muttered. "A likely story!" He whirled about in time to see Nathan reel and almost topple to the ground.

"Halt!" he shouted, his hand on his gun. "You won't get away with this, young man! You're sot drunk, that's what you are. Likely giving me a made-up story about this little girl. I've a mind to take you to the hoosegow."

"Take me wherever you please, sir, but please take care of the child," Nathan said wearily. "She's suffered long exposure—and she's as cold as a wedge."

"Where you headed?"

"To Mrs. Birmingham's boardinghouse, sir, if I can make it there."

"You be sure and go straight there, because I'll be checking up on you to see if you are telling the truth."

"Please do."

Nathan turned to look back at the child. Her eyes sought his for an explanation of his desertion. He would rather have gone to prison than to turn the girl into the hands of this brusque character.

But Nathan Parsons had no choice; he was a sick man and he knew it. He prayed that somehow Becky would understand.

Chapter Sixteen

Miracles

"*W*here am I?" With great effort, Arthur opened one eye to find Lucy bathing his head with a damp cloth. The other eye wouldn't open. Embarrassed, he tried to get up.

"The doctor said you must keep quiet and still, Arthur." Lucy controlled her voice in an effort to comfort him, placing a gentle hand on his arm. "Thank God, you're waking up."

"What happened? It's time to get Dessie from school. I must go!"

"I'm sure someone is taking care of Mrs. Gibson. Just rest."

The vacant eyes took on small bits of recollection. "But . . . why am I here at your house?"

"You were in an accident. The bridge gave way . . ."

"The bridge? What bridge?"

"Over Dry Gulch. Too much rain."

"What was I doing on the bridge?"

"I suppose you were going to school for Mrs. Gibson. School let out early . . ."

"When was that?"

"That was yesterday."

Arthur was silent, searching her face. "I'm . . . I'm starting to remember. Was Dave . . . er, Mr. Parsons on the bridge, too?"

"I . . . didn't see anybody. I heard the crack and ran back . . . and saw your horse dragging your gig out of the mud. You . . . were injured."

Arthur furrowed his brow in deep thought. Suddenly his eyes grew wild. He fought at the restraining quilt that covered him, determined to get off the daybed, then sank back in despair when his strength failed him.

"Everything is all right, Arthur," crooned Lucy, but the terror in his eyes only intensified. "The doctor said if you gained consciousness within twenty-four hours . . ."

"Where's . . . where's *Becky?*"

"I suppose she's with Mrs. Gibson . . ."

"No, I was taking her to Dessie when . . ."

Lucy's mouth went dry. She had forgotten that he had kept Becky at home yesterday. Now she remembered that Mrs. Gibson left the child in Arthur's care throughout the rainy week while he was off work.

"I . . . didn't see Becky. Did you have her with you?"

"Yes! Oh, Lucy! Oh, God! I *did* have Becky with me! What happened to Becky?" The voice, first prayerful, became pleading and finally hysterical.

"I don't know, Arthur." The words were a tremulous whisper.

"Mama and Papa sent me here to *protect* Dessie and Becky. Now if Becky is drowned, I'm responsible. I've

110

failed . . ."

A frightened Lucy found no words of encouragement. If indeed Becky was in the shay with Arthur, her body must be floating somewhere in the murky waters downstream. She might never be found.

Tears formed in Arthur's swollen eyes and were matched by Lucy's sympathetic ones. Together they wept unashamedly.

"Do you know how to pray, Lucy?"

Lucy nodded. "Yes. I pray every night. Mrs. Gibson and I used to pray together. She taught me so much about . . . being a real Christian."

"Then let's pray for . . . about Becky."

Mrs. Wells came with broth for the invalid and stopped at the door. Moved by the tender sight, she tiptoed back to the kitchen. Mayor Wells returned from a council meeting and found the two praying. He supposed that the tears were tears of thankfulness, suspecting his daughter's fondness for the handsome brother of Mrs. Gibson. He stood reverently, waiting with congratulations that Arthur had "come to."

When Lucy turned a distressed face to her father, he was taken aback. "Is Arthur in a great deal of pain, Lucy?"

"Pain of heart, Father. He says Mrs. Gibson's little girl, Becky, was with him in the buggy at the time of the accident. He . . . doesn't know what happened to her when the bridge collapsed."

Mayor Well's face went white. "I'll . . . we'll call a search." He ran for the front door like a madman, pausing only long enough to ask, "Where is the child's mother, Lucy?"

111

"I . . . we don't know, Father."

Arthur refused to be consoled. "We have prayed, and now we must trust God's great wisdom, Arthur." Lucy placed her small, feminine hand on his large bronzed one. "He . . . He knows what is best."

"Becky is all Dessie had, Lucy. It seems that all her life she has been 'losing.' We had a little crippled foster sister Dessie's age named Effie that she loved dearly. She taught her to read, shared her toys with her and defended her against the whole cruel world. She hoped to graduate with Effie, but Effie . . . left and Dessie had to graduate alone . . ."

Arthur paused, but Lucy knew that his story was not complete.

"Dessie never had many beaux; just one sweetheart when she was pretty young, my brother Matthew told me. She waited late in life and finally married Walt, our neighbor's son, and moved here. Mama and Papa didn't want her to move away from Brazos Point. Mama vowed that even the name of Limestone Gap sounded like a funeral dirge. And sure enough, Walt lost his life here last year, leaving Dessie a widow. Dessie was always so *good;* I can't understand all this tragedy. Now if she has lost Becky, I . . . I don't believe she'll be able to stay here. Nor will I."

So the loss would be far reaching. Not only was Becky lost, but Lucy would lose her beloved teacher . . . and the man she loved. Every emotion in her slender body rebelled at the new and frightening thought.

"Is there anyway I . . . anyone can get a message across the river to Dessie?" Arthur asked abruptly.

"Probably not this morning. Papa said they would try

to raft across in the afternoon if the weather holds clear."

"I need to get Dessie word . . ."

The brass door-knocker sounded, loud and urgent. Lucy jumped. "Excuse me, Arthur, while I get the door. Mother is back in the kitchen."

Arthur closed his good eye, agony nailing his spirit to the tree of grief. "Oh, Dessie, I'm sorry!" he groaned helplessly. Oh, that death would have taken him instead! It mattered not to him if he ever recovered.

Overcome by sorrow, he paid little heed to Lucy's surprise cry at the front door.

"A man that seemed to be intoxicated brought this girl to me," the night watchman explained to the speechless Lucy as he held Becky's hand awkwardly. "He said to bring her to the mayor's house. I hope, miss, that it's not a kidnapping case. But at least, the child is safe and not murdered. And I'll check on that drunk. He said, miss, that the little girl belonged to the schoolteacher. Would you happen to know if this is true?"

Becky, her countenance ravaged with hunger and exhaustion, smiled tiredly up at Lucy.

"Yes." Lucy regained her voice enough to speak the single word.

"You'll see, then, that she is properly situated with her family?"

"We'll be glad to take care of the matter, sir." Lucy's vocabulary returned.

A relieved look spread over the marshal's face, as if an unpleasant obligation had been duly paid. He bowed stiffly and hurried off the porch, apparently fearing lest he be arrested by other complications.

Lucy led Becky directly to the daybed where Arthur

lay. With the miraculous answer to prayer standing beside her, she found herself too choked to speak.

But Becky wasted no time speaking up. Seeing Arthur, she quipped, "I'm *so* hungry, Arthur!"

Arthur opened the eye that gave him sight, staring unbelievingly as though he saw an angel. "Becky! Where have you been?"

"In the water. It was so cold."

"How did you get out?"

"Nathan got me out."

"Nathan? Nathan who?"

Becky shrugged her tiny shoulders. "I don't know Nathan who. Just Nathan."

"Do you know anyone by the name of Nathan, Lucy?"

"No, I don't, Arthur."

"A stranger must have fished her from the river."

"He was not a stranger; he was Nathan," corrected Becky with mild irritation.

"Perhaps it was an angel," offered Lucy.

"Let's go home, Arthur. I'm hungry and I want to see Mommy," insisted the child.

"You and Arthur will have to eat and get strong before you can go home," Lucy told her. "Mother'll bring some soup."

"Are you sick, Arthur?" queried Becky.

"I felt mighty bad before you came, Becky—bad enough to die—but I'm feeling mighty good now."

He reached for Lucy's hand.

Chapter Seventeen

A Changed Man

"*H*ow much farther to Limestone Gap, sir?" young Jay Cunningham asked the dour stage driver.

"About two more hours, sonny."

"My daddy'll be there waiting, sir."

"Uh-huh."

Beatrice's hands shook as she pulled the worn message from her tattered handbag once again. She had wept tears of joy when she found it in her mailbox. "You're a fool, Beatrice, to go traipsing across the country after a reckless bum," her mother scolded, but Beatrice kept packing. Now old doubts crowded in. Was this merely another trick of her irresponsible husband to wound her heart afresh? Would he even be there when she got to journey's end? She had spent the savings in the sugar bowl—the money for next month's rent—to purchase the ticket to Limestone Gap for herself, Jay and Joy.

"Dear Beatrice," he had written in his illiterate scrawl, "I've had a change o' heart. I am working here in a place called Limestone Gap and makin' a fare sum o' money. Enough fer us all to live on. If you can find it in yore heart to fergive me and bring the children and come to me, I will try hard to make a good husband and father. I do not want to be a no count rascal er a selfish brute er a infadel er a spineless sissy. I want to be a man. Yours truly, Slats."

What had come over him she did not know, but being a forgiving sort, she was willing to give him another chance if he meant business. Besides, the children still cried themselves to sleep missing their daddy. Neither curious stares nor sympathetic wagging of heads deterred her; like Esther of old, she put her life on the line, and if she perished . . .well, she just perished. So be it.

Arthur had only been back to work a few days when the owner of the quarries made him a straw boss over his area of work. Slats and Dink Cunningham fell in his assigned crew. He kept his relationship with Slats strictly business, remembering the recent confrontation that still made him angry when he thought of it.

Thus, when Slats Cunningham sought him out one afternoon, it came as a surprise. Shifting from foot to foot, the gauche worker stuttered and stammered.

"Mr. Harris . . ." he faltered, almost losing heart. "Could I please be 'cused from work early t'day?"

"Are you ill?"

Slats's red face added more color. "No sir, I ain't ill. Y'see Beatrice an' my two childern 'er s'pose to be on th' evenin' coach, an' I wanted to tidy up a little afore I went to meet them."

How many times had Slats used this excuse or a similar one to evade work? Being a new foreman, Arthur had no way of knowing what ploys the man habitually used. Dare he risk his own position by trusting a man who had never proved trustworthy?

"Please, sir?"

"How much time do you need?"

" 'Bout an hour off t'day . . .an' all day tomorra."

"Someone will have to do your work."

"That's what I was afeared. An' nobody ain't offerin'." Slats looked uncomfortable. "An' I can't afford to lose my job with my fam'ly comin'."

Something in Slats' artless appeal moved Arthur. "Go on. I'll take your place myself," he said.

"I'm shore beholdin' to you, Mr. Harris."

"Forget it."

Dink Cunningham sought Arthur out at noon the next day as Arthur spread his lunch on a rock. "I want to thank ye fer lettin' my brother off'n work," he said.

"Did his family arrive?"

"They did, Mr. Harris. Y'know, at first I thought 'twas jest another o' Slats's tricks, jest an excuse to get outta work an' go on anuther drinkin' bender. He ain't never been much 'count in 'is life, y'know. 'Twas perty sorry o' him to leave Beatrice an' th' kids back in Aspermont in th' first place. An' I tole him so agin an' agin. But he always had ways o' lyin' to shuck his responsibility, an' I jest figgered this was one more lie. So when I got off'n work myself yesterday, I follered 'im jest to see.

"When I got to th' station, there she was—Beatrice—an' those two perty childern sittin' so prim an' proper-like on th' bench at th' coach stop. I hid myself an' watched to see what would happen when Slats driv up.

"Well, sir, up he came, all spruced out like he was goin' sparkin' fer th' first time with 'is girlfriend, in 'is

117

silk top hat an' fancy suit. Beatrice, she looked an' then she looked agin—an' then she flung 'erself into 'is arms. It was th' pertiest sight I ever did see." Dink stopped to wipe his eyes with the back of his dirty hand. "One kid latched onto 'is right leg an' th' t'othern grabbed 'is left. An' Slats looked jest as pleased as a settin' hen."

Dink brushed away another tear. "They shore make a fetchin' little fam'ly."

"I'm happy for him." Arthur's comment was genuine.

"Mr. Harris, somethin' changed in Slats 'bout two weeks ago. 'Twas durin' th' week we layed off'n work on account o' th' bad rains. He laid off'n 'is bottle an' stayed plum sober. He came atalkin' to me, an' not makin' real good sense, ifn you know what I mean. He said he was tired o' bein' a no 'count rascal. 'Well,' says I, 'a body can change ifn he wants to desperate 'nough.'

" 'Well, brother, I'm wantin' to that bad,' he said. Then he began tellin' 'bout what a selfish brute he had been to think on 'isself an' not considerin' 'is two childern needin' bread. Then he got to quotin' some Scriptures, tho' he never did put no stock in th' Bible afore, an' I know fer shore he ain't been to no church lately. He said th' Good Book said anybody that wouldn't take keer o' their own fam'ly was worser than a infidel. Does th' Bible say those words, Mr. Harris?"

"It says it."

"Slats said he'd never agin live so's anybody could call 'im a spineless sissy—never agin. I don't know who called 'is bluff, but I'll ferever be beholdin' to whoever did it. Shore eases my load."

Arthur's mind somersaulted back to the conversation at the front door of Dessie's house when his anger at Slats almost got the best of him.

"He's truly a changed man, Mr. Harris. I ain't heared 'im say a cuss word on th' job all this week, an' he used to cuss at ever'thing that went wrong. He had a bad mouth on 'im.

"But here's what he said. He said, 'I'm gonna make a real man outta myself, Dink.' I didn't put no real stock in his words, figgerin' they was idle an' would wear off with time an' mind-changin'. But when he wrote that letter an' sent fer Beatrice an' those kids to come to the Gap, I knew he meant business an' warn't jest playin' around.

"I went over last night to th' new house he rented to greet my sister-in-law, an' Slats asked me to bring you a message."

"Me?"

"Yes, sir. He said to thank you fer all you'd done fer him an' to tell you that you an' yorn er welcome to come an' see him an' his family any time. He wanted you to see 'is boy an' 'is girl. He's mighty proud o' that little fam'ly o' his'n!"

Never judge a man too harshly, he had told Dessie. And he had almost broken his own rule. *There's so much bad in the best of us and so much good in the worst.* Papa was right.

That was the beautiful part of humanity, Arthur reflected. God created them so they could be changeable. And when they couldn't do the changing themselves, He would help them. Even if he had to use an angry "prophet."

"If you see Slats before I do, Mr. Cunningham, give him my sincere congratulations," Arthur heard himself saying. "And I'll try my best to pay him a visit one of these days and meet his fine family."

Chapter Eighteen

The Watchman's Inquisition

"Can I help you, sir?" Mrs. Birmingham, seeing the officer's shiny badge, expected trouble. Who could it be this time?

Probably Tom Reeder. He had been jailed for barroom brawls before. She had threatened to turn him out on the streets, but he promised faithfully to mend his errant ways. And besides, he always paid his rent on time.

Or it could be "Tiny" Dobson, her six-foot-six giant of a boarder, who sometimes forgot his profane tongue in the presence of ladies. Usually, he paid his fine and watched his language for a few days. He was quite a source of revenue for the law department.

Keeping a boardinghouse for men was no picnic, but any one of them would fight for her at the drop of a hat. She felt secure, made good money, and was quick to jump to the defense of any one of her roomers just as she prepared to do now.

The officer removed his hat. "I'm Thurman Boles, night watchman over at the Gap, ma'am. I'm checking

121

on a man who said he roomed here at your boarding-house.''

"Yes?" Mrs. Birmingham raised her brows archly, bristling like a cornered porcupine.

"Do you have a man registered here by the name of Parsons . . . Dave Parsons?

"I do, sir. He's been here since the summer past."

"I need to speak to him. He left our community a few days ago staggering drunk."

"Oh, you must be mistaken, officer. Mr. Parsons doesn't drink. He's the superintendent for all the county schools and has an impecable record of behavior, I can assure you. He's one of my very best tenants."

"Just as I thought."

"You thought what?" Mrs. Birmingham demanded. She could be callous for a lady.

"The man lied to me. He wasn't Dave Parsons at all. When he gave me the name, he almost forgot and gave his own name instead. I do need to inform the honorable superintendent that someone has been impersonating him—using his name."

"Of course. But what do you suppose would have been the culprit's purpose in feigning himself to be our good school official?"

"I wouldn't know. I'm sure we have a criminal case on our hands here. I don't normally give out details, but since you were named as the landlady, you might need to know the details in order to help us."

"Please inform me." Mrs. Birmingham relished being "in on things."

Watchman Boles lowered his voice importantly, casting his eyes about to assure himself that no eavesdroppers lurked nearby. "The man had a little girl in tow—perhaps three or four years old at most. The poor thing was dripping wet, shivering with cold, and looked like a drowned rat. He put the child in my care, instructing me to take her to the mayor of our city. Then he lurched off, saying he was going 'home' to Mrs. Birmingham's boardinghouse."

"How terrible! And you suspect a kidnapping attempt?"

"Wouldn't you?"

"I would."

"Couldn't have been anything less."

"I hate it that my rooms have been incriminated . . . I hope it doesn't damage my business . . ."

"Oh, you'll have my word that we'll keep this hush-hush."

"Mr. Parsons will surely be grieved to know that such a character chose his good name to use in connection with the crime."

"May I speak with the superintendent myself?"

"I haven't seen him about for two or three days. He must be gone on one of his school rounds. Unless . . ."

"Unless what?"

"Unless he came in after I went to sleep last evening and hasn't arisen yet this morning."

"You'll check his room for me?"

"I'll check."

Officer Boles seated himself in the cluttered parlor, studying various religious pictures on the walls to pass the time. Jesus holding a sheep. The scene of the newborn Christ in the manger. The crucifixion. The paintings failed to hold his attention for long, however. His mind turned inward.

He envisioned himself famous, with his name splashed across the newspapers and spoken on the lips of both rich and poor for his ingenuity in breaking the kidnapping case. He'd certainly know the man if he saw him again, and he'd search until he found him. A tall man with dark brown eyes, a crease in his chin, a cowlick wave in the middle of a heavy head of blackish hair. He'd be an easy one to identify anywhere.

Mrs. Birmingham was gone so long that Officer Boles began to wonder if she had deserted him. When she did return, worry lines distorted her aging features.

"Did you find Mr. Parsons?"

"I found him," she said nervously. "I knocked on his door and got no response. Then I heard a low moan. I went in and found him delirious."

The marshal gasped. "Sounds like a frame-up. Someone has tried to kill him. Probably the man that used his name!"

"There are no obvious injuries, but he is burning up with a fever. I don't know how long he has been in this condition. Too long, I'm afraid. I hope he can . . .be saved."

"Shall I go for a doctor, Mrs. Birmingham? It's important that he lives so that he can testify."

"Will you please? I'll see if I can get some water down him. His lips are swollen almost double and cracked."

"I'll come on back with the doctor in case Mr. Parsons rallies. You understand that it's highly important that we get all the information we can as quickly as possible!"

Mrs. Birmingham scowled at the night watchman.

"What is important, Mr. Boles, is that we get our county school superintendent back to health."

Mr. Boles, half afraid of this formidable woman, skittered off to find the county's most renowned doctor.

Mrs. Birmingham posted herself beside Dave Parsons, determined to fight for his life to the bitter end. She had seen more than one person die in her sixty-two years, and she knew this one was knocking on death's door now. His labored breathing and flighty pulse told her a story she did not like. She pulled more covers from the quiltbox and wrapped his icy feet in flannel.

"I don't know much about you, David Parsons," she said to the unheeding man, holding his inert hand, "but you're a good man. And I'm not going to let you die."

His eyelids fluttered and he tried to mouth a single word. She bent her ear low to hear his whisper. "Becky . . ."

Could Becky be a wife, a sweetheart? She had no address of next of kin save that of his father in Louisiana. He had never mentioned anyone named Becky. But sometimes at the point of death, lost love came back and broken relationships were mended.

She moved close to his ear. "Is Becky your wife?" He shook his head. "Is she your sweetheart?" Again he shook his head, then faded into unconsciousness again.

The doctor came hurriedly, along with Officer Boles.

"He's . . . bad, doctor." Mrs. Birmingham met him at the door, leading the way to Nathan's room. The officer disrespectfully followed, hoping to find clues in his self-appointed investigation.

At the sight of Nathan, Mr. Boles gasped.

"I told you he was very ill, Mr. Boles."

125

"It . . . I . . . This is the man that gave me the child. This is . . . Dave Parsons."

"I forbid you to utter a word about this until he is well enough to speak for himself—if he lives to tell his side of the story," Mrs. Birmingham ordered. "Or I'll have *you* arrested for slander." She pushed him toward the door and dismissed him with an authority that dwarfed his.

"Becky," the sick man had whispered. He had a little girl with him, Mr. Boles said. And she was "wet as a drowned rat." Dave's clothing lay crumpled on the floor, gathering mildew. Clothing that were mud-caked and mossy. Yes, there was a story behind it all.

A story that might never be told.

Illness

"I haven't seen Dave since before the flood," Arthur mentioned off-handedly one night after supper. "I hope he didn't get washed away."

Dessie laid aside her embroidering. "He hasn't been by the classroom checking up on Becky and me, either."

"He usually comes into town on Saturdays. He claims the boardinghouse gives him claustrophobia. I think it's mostly loneliness that brings him. He hasn't been in for two Saturdays now."

"He . . . lives in a *boardinghouse?*"

Arthur berated himself for unwittingly giving out the information. "Yes."

"Does his *whole family* live in the boardinghouse?"

"He doesn't have a family . . . now."

Dessie grabbed mismatched puzzle pieces from the shelf of memory, getting parts from the wrong puzzle. Could this be the man that Arthur told her planned to visit her and propose marriage? The man with the shady past? The married man with two children somewhere, trying to cover his sins? The man that Arthur said wouldn't be good for her . . . or Becky? Is this why he had changed his name from Nathan to Dave? Who else would Arthur know intimately enough to learn of his plans? It could be no other. *Oh, Nathan . . . not you!*

"You don't suppose he's . . . resigned and moved away?" Dessie lowered her head over the stitches so that her face would be veiled and Arthur could not possibly detect her thoughts.

"No. The mayor would know it if he had."

Dessie threaded her needle with two strands of gold embroidery thread to make French knots in the middle of her flower, meditating more on Nathan than on the pillowslip pattern. She could not imagine Arthur taking up with a man of such poor character. What if the school board learned of his past?

"You know, Dessie, there are so many things about the accident on the bridge that I can't quite remember. And Dave is one of them."

"Why Dave?"

"Somewhere in the back of my mind—or perhaps it was a dream—I thought I saw Dave on the bridge with me when it collapsed."

"Don't you think Lucy would have seen him if he had been on the bridge?"

"I . . . suppose so."

Dark threads of alarm wove themselves into Dessie's thought pattern, but she hid her emotions from Arthur. What if Nathan . . . left the country unannounced? Then she chided herself for caring so much whether this man whose background she knew so little about stayed or went. She dared not ask Arthur further questions, lest he suspect her motives.

When yet another Saturday made history and still Dave failed to show up in the Gap, Arthur became concerned. "I'm going over and see about Dave," he told Dessie on Sunday.

"How far is it?"

"About ten miles. Do you and Becky want to go along?"

Dessie hesitated. "I'd enjoy the ride, but remember, Dave doesn't know that you and I are acquainted. And I think we'd better keep it that way until the school conflict is settled."

"Your word is law."

Arthur called for Dave Parsons at Mrs. Birmingham's place of business, giving his name and explaining that he was a personal friend.

"Just a minute, young man." The overprotective proprietress disappeared and soon returned.

"Mr. Parsons will see you in his room, Mr. Harris. He's been so ill that I take it upon myself to screen his visitors. The nosy night watchman from the Gap has been here several times, but I always turn him away."

Arthur followed her to "Dave's" room. The sight that met him gave him a dreadful shock. Nathan peered from sunken eyes, his bones visible through sallow skin. His face evaporated into teeth when he smiled.

"What happened, old buddy?"

"Had a fight with death."

"Looks like you won."

"Doctor says I'm winning. I . . . hope I am. It's been a . . . tough battle."

"Been sick long?"

"It's hard to remember when I *wasn't* sick."

"I haven't seen you around since the great flood."

"No."

"Were you in our area when the water of the 'dry' gulch jumped its banks?"

"Yes, I was."

"I've something that's been bothering my mind for days, Dave."

"Get it off."

"Did you know about my accident?"

"Yes."

"Were you on the bridge with me when it let go?"

"Yes, I was."

"Then you were injured, too?"

"Not really. Just got cold and wet and developed pneumonia."

"You were able to swim out?"

"Washed down the river about a mile or so first."

"The strangest thing happened, Dave. I had Des . . . the schoolteacher's little girl with me when I wrecked. She was evidently thrown out into the water. Someone brought her to the mayor's house the next day still wet and hungry."

Nathan looked at the ceiling, mentally tracing the water circles caused by an old roof leak. He dared not look at Arthur.

"I'm . . . glad she was returned safely. I had wondered about her many times."

"But that's not all the story. When we asked her how she got out of the river, she said 'Nathan got me out.' None of us know anyone by the name of Nathan. We can't imagine who it could have been. Lucy suggested that it may have been an angel. That explanation is intriguing, but I never read of any angels in the Bible named Nathan."

"I don't expect it really matters who got her out, just so she got out alive. That was a miracle. Did the exposure make her ill?"

"She's as fit as a fiddle."

"Were . . . you badly injured yourself?"

"A beam from the bridge knocked me out for several hours, but nothing serious. I had a good nurse." Arthur laughed.

"It wouldn't have been Lucy Wells?"

"Yes."

"I think she has her clock set for you, Arthur." Nathan's bloodshot eyes crinkled at the corners.

"I'll try not to let it wind down."

"But how did you know I was ill?"

"Missed you around town. I guess others have missed you, too. Mrs. Birmingham said Mr. Boles had been over checking on you several times lately."

"Mister who?"

"Mr. Boles. Thurman Boles. The Gap's night patrol."

"Oh, I see."

"He a good friend of yours?"

"I've never met him but once."

"You must have impressed him."

"I can't imagine why he'd want to see me. I'd promised him a little money for an errand he ran for me, but I sent a lad into town with that before I . . . lost consciousness."

"Is there anything I can do for you, Dave?"

"You can pray."

"I've been doing that, even before I knew you were laid up."

"I really would like to have a long talk with you when I'm stronger."

"Any time, Dave. My time is yours."

"When I felt sure I wasn't going to make it, I made God some promises. And I know I have to keep my end of the bargain."

"He'll sure keep His end."

"I'm not worried about Him doing His part. I have to give Him a chance, though."

Chapter Twenty

A Conflicting Story

*A*rthur hitched his horse to the post. Unfolding his long legs from the confines of the buggy, he alighted and made his way along the cobblestone path to the neat rock house.

Before he could lift the iron clapper to announce his presence, a small face appeared in the doorway. No one need tell Arthur that this was Slatson Cunningham's son. The resemblance was uncanny.

"Hello, sir." Jay's manners bespoke careful training. "May I tell Father that you are here?"

"Please."

Slats came smiling, dressed immaculately in serge trousers and a color-coordinated twill shirt. "Mr. Harris!" he greeted enthusiastically. "How nice o' you to call. May I present my fam'ly? Beatrice . . . Joy . . ."

A beautiful lady, slender and prematurely gray, appeared as if by magic. Beside her stood a small likeness of herself. What once must have been worry lines on the gentle face of Beatrice, put there by a thoughtless husband, were now converted to smile lines.

"Bee, this is my boss at th' quarry, Arthur Harris. I've had a lot o' bosses in my day, but this one is th' best I ever had. He's a Christian."

Beatrice's face glowed. "Thank you, Mr. Harris, for what you have done for my dear husband . . . and for all of us. It's a pleasure to meet you." Joy and Jay nodded.

"Mrs. Cunningham, it is an honor to be foreman over a fellow who is making a real man of himself." Arthur could not have voiced this compliment a month ago; now he found himself compelled to speak. "You can be proud of him."

"Oh, I am, sir." Happiness shown in her warm gray-blue eyes. "I'm sure he always . . . meant well."

"No, Beatrice," contradicted Slats humbly, "I didn't always mean well. I was totally selfish . . . until Mr. Harris showed me my error."

"I . . . we all make mistakes. It's not the past that counts, it's what we do with today . . . and tomorrow," Arthur said slowly, gently closing the subject.

"How is your family, Mr. Harris?" asked Beatrice politely.

"I live with my widowed sister and small niece, Mrs. Cunningham. And they are both well, thank you."

"I've been intending to ask you, Mr. Harris, about the report of your niece being kidnapped," Slats said.

"Kidnapped? Becky kidnapped?" Arthur started in alarm. "Today?"

"No, no." Slats held up a restraining hand. "I didn't mean to frighten you. It was back during th' river risin'. They tell me th' night watchman o' the Gap has been lookin' fer a man named Parsons in connection with th'

134

crime."

"Parsons?" Arthur looked perplexed. The news . . . the name . . . nothing made sense.

"Yes. I b'lieve th' first name is Dave."

"Dave Parsons?"

"I b'lieve that's th' name, sir. I tried to listen carefully so's I'd know it ifn I ran acrost th' kidnapper perchance."

"I . . . I'm afraid I don't understand." Arthur shook his head in bewilderment. "My niece, Becky, was safe and well with her mother when I left the house early this morning. She has never been kidnapped. When the quarries were shut down, I kept her while my sister taught school. Unless . . . unless a stranger saw her in the buggy with me and thought *I* had abducted her." Arthur paused. "Dave Parsons is the county school superintendent and a personal friend of mine. I just left his place and came here."

"I'm not real well acquainted here, so I didn't recognize th' name as anyone in our town. But th' report is that some man brought th' child drippin' wet into town about daylight one mornin' from th' direction o' th' river. He voluntarily handed her over to th' watchman an' requested that he take her to th' mayor's house. Th' security officers became suspicious . . ."

"Oh, I'm sure it wasn't Dave Parsons."

"Then . . . none of th' story is true?"

Arthur chuckled. "Well, it's partly true. But things do get out of context in a hurry. We suppose that Becky was thrown into the river when the bridge toppled, though nobody actually saw what happened. She was in the gig with me at the time of the accident. I was struck in the head by a falling beam, so I can't vouch for what hap-

pened myself. But I was at the mayor's house recouper-
ating when Mr. Boles brought Becky there. Becky told
me that a man by the name of Nathan rescued her from
the river. The only thing is, we don't know of anyone by
that name. It must have been a passerby. Do we have a
Nathan working at the quarries?"

"Not to my knowledge, sir. I hear that Mr. Boles says
that th' man who brought th' child to him was dead
drunk . . . staggerin' an' bleary-eyed. Even ifn his motives
t'ward th' child was right, Mr. Boles wants to find 'im
an' charge 'im with public drunkeness."

"Well, Mr. Boles had better be looking for a Nathan
somebody rather than Dave Parsons. He's got his leads
all wrong; Dave would never drink a drop."

"You don't s'pose someone would've used th' superintendent's name, do you, Mr. Harris?"

"That's possible, but it doesn't seem . . . logical."

"Perhaps you should inform yore friend about it."

"Yes . . . or talk to Mr. Boles."

"Had your niece ever heard of anyone by the name
of Nathan, Mr. Harris? A relative, perhaps?" suggested
Mrs. Cunningham. "Could she have just plucked the name
out of her memory?"

"No, I don't suppose she had ever heard the name
in her life."

"How old is she?"

"She's not quite four, but she's extraordinarily sharp
for her age, with a knack for remembering. If she said
Nathan, then the man's name was Nathan, I'm sure."

"I'll pass the clue on at the queries, Mr. Harris," Slats
promised.

Arthur cut his stay short, leaving with the satisfaction that a metamorphoses had taken place in the life of Slatson Cunningham—and perhaps he had had a small part in the transformation. *It takes some boys many years to grow up,* Papa used to say, *and some never do.* Slats Cunningham had finally grown up.

Dessie would wonder what kept him away so long. She would be waiting on him to have the evening devotion. He need not tell her he had visited the "no-account" man, now a happy family provider, that he had warned her of. The man he had described to her no longer existed. And if she asked about his visit with Dave, he would just tell her Dave had been ill—no need to bother her with details.

But Dessie asked no questions other than to inquire if he had found the superintendent.

"Yes," he teased. "It looks like the superintendent will be around for a while yet, Dessie. I guess your job is still in jeopardy!"

A relief, rather than the frown Arthur expected, brushed across her face.

Chapter Twenty-One

Dismissed

*T*he chalk scratched across the blackboard as Dessie wrote the arithmetic figures in even, vertical rows, her back to the class.

"Grades four and five, please get out your tablets and . . ." Dessie sensed rather than saw the movement at her side. When she wheeled about to look, Becky had leaped from her chair, run the length of the building, and caught the tall man who had entered by the legs.

Dessie, reeling with shock and embarrassment, stood gaping helplessly. Becky had never acted so disorderly before. She looked up to apologize to this emaciated visitor, and when their eyes met, she recognized him as Nathan Parsons. He had lost at least thirty pounds, and he looked ten years older. What had happened to him?

"Becky!" she scolded, finding her tongue. "Go back to your seat right now!"

With a hurt glance at her mother, Becky reluctantly backed away, never taking her eyes from Nathan. "I wanted to say thank you," she reproached, but Dessie failed to comprehend the child's logic.

Nathan lowered his intense brown eyes self-consciously. When he regained his composure, he asked, "Could the class be recessed while I have a conference with you, Mrs. Gibson?"

"Yes, sir." Dessie knew the day of reckoning had come and tried to brace for the inevitable.

"Would it be all right if the child went out with an older pupil?" With great effort, Nathan pulled his attention from Becky.

"Yes, sir." She turned to Lucy Wells. "Please take Becky outdoors and take care of her."

A puzzled Lucy smiled coyly. "Yes, Mrs. Gibson."

When the students had filed out quietly, Nathan sat down across the desk from her, breathing hard. She noticed that his hands shook as he fumbled with a button on his jacket. Something was different about Nathan Parsons—something besides his skeletal frame. Dessie tried to place it. A quick face-search brought the answer. The hardness that once possessed his eyes was no longer there.

"Mrs. Gibson," he began, with effort, "About Beck . . . the child. Is her presence in the classroom today an isolated incident?"

"No, sir."

"Your nursemaid is sick perhaps?"

It seemed to Dessie's flustered mind that Nathan actually sought a legitimate way to excuse Becky's being there.

"I bring her every day, sir. I made it clear that I would have to bring her with me before I accepted the teaching position."

"But when I came the last time, she wasn't in evidence."

"She was with Ar . . . a relative."

"Couldn't this relative keep her every day?"

"No, sir, he couldn't. He works. He only kept her during the rain when his job at the quarry was shut down."

"I deeply regret to inform you, Mrs. Gibson, that I must terminate your teaching here at the Gap school. I understand that your academic standing is excellent and that you maintain a good rapport with your pupils. But rules are rules, and in order to live with my conscience, I must see that they are enforced."

"I understand, sir." To evade his piercing eyes, Dessie looked at the floor. His scuffed rawhide boots seemed out of character with the rest of his attire but fitting for the man himself.

"I'm sure you do understand. When I signed the contract with the county, I promised to play a fair game. You . . . wouldn't want me to do otherwise."

The ultimatum sounded more like a weary apology than a command.

"When . . . ?" Dessie faltered, not knowing how to ask the pressing question.

"This is Thursday. Tomorrow will be your last day. I'll pull in a substitute until we can find a permanent replacement."

One more day to get Annie Rushing into yet another book. Jacob could recite quite well now. This was Lucy's last year anyhow; she'd manage . . .

"Thank you, sir, for allowing me to teach this long. It has been a . . . pleasure. And I beg your pardon for my daughter's actions today."

When she told Arthur about the incident that night, he refused to allow her to be distressed about the loss of her job.

"Now Dessie," he said in his Papa-like voice, "I came to the Gap to take care of you and Becky. I have a good job, making more in a month than I ever thought I'd make in a whole year. We'll manage fine."

"I appreciate that, Arthur. I really do. But you need to be saving your income for the day you'll have a home of your own."

"That'll all take care of itself, Sis. You've told me yourself that if we belong to God, He's monitoring the happenings of our life on this earth. He gave you the job . . . and He has taken it away. We'll give thanks in all things."

"I'll . . . sure miss my pupils."

"And they'll miss you. Especially Lucy. But I've got a feeling this thing isn't over. The mayor will rise to arms for you, Dessie. He'll put up a fight. I just don't know who'll win."

"I don't want the mayor to give the superintendent any static over me."

"You have very little control over the outcome, Dessie. You . . . we all knew from the start that the showdown was coming sooner or later . . . and it's here."

The mayor, as Arthur predicted, wasted no time jumping into the waters troubled by a county agent. In one of his platform speeches, he declared that the county had no right to dictate local statutes and pledged himself to defend the city's independence. Arthur suspected that he welcomed this issue as an opportunity to prove his worthiness.

142

Lucy delivered the letter summoning Dessie to a meeting the following week that would decide her fate . . . as if it was not already decided. The case promised to be a highly charged one with heated arguments on each side. The newspapers took up the story and ran with it. Dessie wished she could call the whole matter off with a simple explanation that she felt Mr. Parsons was right to stand by his principles. But it wasn't that easy. The mayor would hear none of it.

Nathan would surely call the state advocates to defend himself. Dessie found herself hoping so.

Nathan. Her mind went back to the fateful Thursday afternoon—to the part she told no one about. She closed her eyes, reliving the scene. She had thanked Nathan for allowing her to teach in the Gap school and apologized for Becky's inordinate actions.

Nathan had turned his head away, then looked back, directly into her eyes. "Please understand, Mrs. Gibson, that I have nothing against the child," he had said, with a kind of magnanimity. "And please . . . don't punish her for . . . what she did."

"You're a good man . . . *Nathan.*" When she lowered her head, a tear dropped onto her polished desk . . . and when she raised it again, he was gone. He must have ran from the room.

Why had she spoken his name?

Chapter Twenty-Two

House Hunting

"*I*'ve got to get out of that boardinghouse," Nathan said to Arthur when they met at the barber shop on Saturday. "Since my illness, Mrs. Birmingham treats me like a ten-year-old child. She wants to know where I'm going and when I'm coming back—and if I took my bitters while I was gone!"

"Besides being slightly on the bossy side," grinned Arthur. "I know. She met me at the door when I came to visit you. She admitted to screening your visitors carefully."

"She means nothing by it, of course," Nathan conceded. "But I've reached the saturation point. I feel the thunder building up. And I want to beat the storm."

"Have you considered a hotel? At least, you'd be your own boss."

"I've never stayed in a hotel that wasn't dingy and overrun with brawling roamers."

"Since I've never stayed in a hotel in my life, I wouldn't know. But coach stops are bad enough. If they're anything like coach houses . . .''

"I'm afraid they are. What I need is a place of my own. And with winter coming on, I need to be here in the Gap; it's the center of my area. That close brush with death gave me a respect for pneumonia. The doctor said I'd have to take care of myself for a while. Another bout with the stuff would snuff me out.''

"Have you looked about for property?''

"I have a list from Mr. Davis, the realtor. Thought I might get you to go along with me since you know the area better than I do. You might know which wells run good water and which are gyps.''

"I'm not that knowledgeable,'' laughed Arthur, "but I'd be glad to go along with you.''

"Mr. Davis has three places listed, and he drew me maps to all three. I told him I wanted on the fringes of town with a little land for a garden. I'd like to get situated before the holidays.''

"I'm ready to go when you are.''

"I've never dreaded winter,'' Nathan said as they started out, "until this year. I believe I miss my . . . little girl worse than I ever have. Winter can be a bleak and lonely time of the year.'' The deciduous trees along the route had shed their covering of green, and a windbreaker felt good.

"Won't you be even lonelier in a house all alone?''

Nathan sighed. "I'm afraid so. But I did have a brainstorm last night . . .''

"How's that?''

"I thought your folks might consent to allowing you to move in with me . . .'' Nathan broke off his sentence, its tone suggesting a question rather than a statement.

"I . . . I'd be glad to if I could. But . . . I'm the man of the house right now."

"I see." Nathan said no more.

Arthur studied the crude map Mr. Davis had drawn up. "Looks like the first place on the list is north of the quarries," he said. "Pretty good soil up that direction. One of the men in my division at work lives out there. A Mr. Cunningham. He just sent for his wife and family from out west and has a place rented in that area. They have two lovely children and would make good neighbors. Might knock the edge off some of your loneliness."

"Sounds good to me. What does it say about the property?"

"Neat rock house. Five acres partly cleared. Spring on place flows year-round."

"Can't beat that."

"I can't quite place it," puzzled Arthur. "The house must be back from the road, hidden by trees. I've traveled the road before, and never noticed . . ."

He pored over the misleading map. They passed the Cunningham place and went a mile farther, but found nothing. "Let me see that map, Arthur."

Nathan traced the thin lines with his finger. "It's that rock house we passed a mile back," he said, straightening.

"That's the Cunningham place."

"They own it?"

"No, they're just renting."

"I guess the owner has decided to sell. That's the only place it can be. Let's stop in and see if the tenants know anything about it."

Beatrice met them at the door wreathed in womanly loveliness. Her crisply starched apron displayed streaks of flour; the spicy smells from the kitchen were enticing.

"This is my friend, Dave Parsons," introduced Arthur. "Is Mr. Cunningham in?"

"I'm sorry, but he isn't, Mr. Harris. He took Jay hunting. They should be back in a couple of hours."

"Would you happen to know, Mrs. Cunningham, if this place is for sale?"

A look akin to pain crossed the sweet face. "Yes, it is, sir. We had hoped to be able to buy it ourselves, but Slats lacks a few more paydays before we can come up with the down payment. Were you . . . wanting to buy it?"

"Mr. Parsons is looking for a place in the Gap. He's our county school superintendent . . ."

"I see." Arthur suspected she hadn't meant for her voice to carry the noticeable tinge of disappointment.

"If . . . if your husband is considering buying it, ma'am, I wouldn't think of evicting you. You have a family and you are already established here; I just live alone and can easily find another place."

The next stop took them farther out to land that bordered on the dry gulch. Evidence that the flood waters had flirted with the door of the unpainted plank house that sat up on cedar posts brought a negative reaction from Nathan. "I don't even want to remember this creek," he said. "And sitting on its banks every day would bring the torment of memories. One flood in a lifetime is enough for me. Let's go."

"We're not having much luck, are we, Dave?"

"Third time charm," he joked. "The next one is bound to be my destiny." He ran his finger over the lines to the third listing.

"What does it say about your destiny?" grilled Arthur.

"It says, 'Ten acres, prime. Solid house. Trees, large shed. Includes most furniture. Good neighborhood, next to mayor.'"

Arthur drew in his breath. *Next to the mayor.* Where could that be? "I can't place that one," he said.

"As much time as you spend visiting the mayor's daughter, I'm surprised," Nathan teased. "You'll be pressing me to buy the place, whatever condition it is in, so you can have another excuse to call on Lucy . . . as if you needed an excuse."

"I don't believe there's any such place," Arthur declared emphatically. "I go up and down that road . . . every day."

"You visit Lucy *that* often?"

Arthur subtly changed the subject. "But if there was such a place, it would be just what you need. Furniture and all. That's unusual."

The wagon passed in front of Dessie's house. "Here it is!" acclaimed Nathan. "Just as Mr. Davis drew it on the map."

"No, that's . . ."

"See that old wagon wheel standing beside the house? When I first passed through the Gap, I had wheel trouble and borrowed it from the lady of the house."

Arthur blinked. What had Dessie said about someone borrowing that wheel? He understood it was an old family friend that she lent it to. Had it been loaned out *twice?*

"I can't imagine why her husband has left it leaning there still," Nathan continued.

"But . . . she doesn't . . " Arthur stopped. He could hardly let Nathan know that this was Dessie's house, that she had no husband, and furthermore that it was not for sale, without revealing his relationship to her—and Dessie had strictly forbidden it. With the "trial" coming up next week, she would want him to remain anonymous.

"Let's go see about it," Nathan urged. "I was here once before, but no one was home. I've got a feeling that this is just the place I'm going to want to buy!"

"But . . ."

Nathan jumped out of the wagon and headed for the door, leaving Arthur nothing to do but follow.

Chapter Twenty-Three

Heart Battle

*D*essie got up from her knees and wiped her eyes, hoping they were not still red from crying, when she heard the rap on the door. The visitor was probably Lucy, and she would understand.

Two men stood at the door. One was Arthur. He gestured behind Nathan, giving her imploring looks which she misinterpreted. He shook his head no, and seemed to be trying to warn her of something, to pass some information to her behind Nathan's back.

What could it be? Then she remembered! Her mind froze into solid panic. Arthur had prewarned her that a man planned on calling . . . a man with the intention of proposing marriage.

This must be what he tried to tell her now with his crude sign language. The time had come. Nathan had fired her and now, thinking her vulnerable and without financial support, he had come to make the proposal.

"Just trust me," Arthur had said, his words crawling back from beyond the flood. She was glad that he made his point clear, because certainly the description Arthur gave of the "no-account" man was out of context with Nathan; all she had to go on was Arthur's word. She must trust her brother's wisdom and not lean on her own deceptive thinking. Women could be swayed by emotion; men knew the weaknesses of their own gender.

"The man has a shady past and would not be good for you . . . or Becky," he'd said. "He's a married man with two children, trying to cover his past." Only Dessie knew that he had attempted to blot out his past by changing his name to Dave. Not even Arthur suspected that.

"If a man comes—*any man*—don't fall for his line. He'll be lying to you." Nathan fit the catagory of "any man," being the first and only man that had come to call on her since Arthur's grim warning.

Thank God, Arthur had come along with the imposter to protect her as he had promised to do. She tossed him a smile that said, "Thank you, Arthur."

She stepped back from the door. If Arthur had not been along, she would not have permitted them entrance.

For the second time in a week, the small form of Becky flew to the towering man and locked her arms about his legs in an intense embrace. Dessie turned a deep shade of red, her mind grappling for an expression of regret for the child's exploit.

"I . . . guess she misses her father," she excused lamely, prying Becky from the man. The excuse made no sense, since Becky had never accosted Arthur, the mayor, or any other male figure in this manner.

Nathan appeared confused. "She's . . . don't be too hard on her, Mrs. Gibson."

"This is my friend, Arthur Harris," the superintendent nodded toward Arthur who bowed slightly at the waist.

Dessie acknowledged the introduction. "Yes, I've met him." The twinkle in her aquamarine eyes almost proved to be Arthur's undoing. He forced a somber hello.

"Of course," brightened Nathan. "Mr. Harris provided transportation for your child the day the bridge broke up."

"Yes, sir."

"What I've come for, Mrs. Gibson, is to check on your property."

A tendril of alarm set off the old warning in Dessie's mind. *He wants your property,* Arthur had said. Nathan was following to the letter the pattern that Arthur had predicted.

A battle between mind and heart raged within Dessie. Her very soul rebelled at the repulsive idea that Nathan was rotten to the core. How could one so conscientious about trite county school rules be a scoundrel in weightier matters? What was the Bible's evaluation of it . . . straining a gnat and swallowing a camel? . . . and he, the son of a preacher, reared by a God-fearing father. *Oh, Nathan!*

Ten years ago, he had been her ideal of manhood. If Arthur only knew how hard it was for her to tear the formidable pedestal from her heart! Of course, Arthur did not suspect—must not know—that her past linked in any way with this man who obviously sought to hide his former life.

She must have been silent, lost in disturbing thoughts, too long. Nathan gave a dry cough and explained. "Mr. Davis gave me the listing. He said some of the furnishings go with the place. Is that correct?" His eyes searched the place, a pleased expression emanating from them.

"Mr. Davis?"

"The realtor."

"Oh, yes . . . the realtor."

Arthur scanned Dessie's face, her bewilderment sewn into the seams of her frown. "We must be at the wrong address, Dave," he suggested. "This lady doesn't even know what you're talking about."

"Has there been a mistake? Was I given the wrong information, Mrs. Gibson?"

Dessie laughed nervously, remembering. "I . . . forget to take the place off the market."

"Off the market?"

"Yes. I listed it back in early August before I took the teaching job. At that time I . . . we planned to return to my home community." She spoke of herself and Becky.

"I see. Then you are not interested in selling at the present time?"

"I . . . really don't know what I'm going to do since I . . ." she looked at Nathan candidly, ". . . lost my job yesterday."

Arthur frowned, trying to send her more secret signals. She understood these facial grimaces to mean she need not sell the place; he would provide for her and Becky in the future. But she wasn't sure this was as she wished it.

"The loss of position put you in . . . financial jeopardy?" Nathan's tone was actually solicitous.

"Oh, no," Dessie replied quickly, wishing no sympathy from this ignoble man. "I am being well taken care of." Frantically, she realized she must ward off this man's marriage proposal any way that she could. She read relief on Arthur's features. She apparently handled the sticky situation to his satisfaction.

"Will you let me know if you decide to sell in the future?" pressed Nathan. "This is the place I want. I like it."

"Yes, I'll let you know."

"Bye-bye, Arthur!" quipped Becky, and Dessie quickly whisked her away lest she reveal his identity to the county school superintendent.

Chapter Twenty-Four

The Council Meeting

"*T*he meeting will now come to order." The mayor opened the meeting in his authoritative and confident voice.

Dessie looked about the room filled with curious people, feeling like the burr under the saddle that caused the horse to pitch. Nathan sat alone, still gaunt and thin, looking peaked and worn. He avoided eye contact with her. She had expected that he would have some reinforcements with him. He had none. This troubled her.

Arthur moved to one side with Lucy and mingled among the spectators. Dessie sat in a center front seat that the mayor had assigned her; Becky sat beside her sedately. In chairs nearby the local school trustees clustered about her as if to defend her against any ridiculous county or state law that might tear her from them. Boles, the night watchman, stole in unobtrusively.

This whole situation is a mistake, Dessie told herself. *And I caused it all by taking the teaching job. I should have returned to Brazos Point, dream or no dream!*

The meeting moved along quickly, the atmosphere heavy with contempt.

"You all know why we are here," boomed the mayor acridly. "This is not a matter of the trivial infraction of a rule. All rules have exceptions. This is a matter of outside agencies dictating to local citizens what they can or cannot do in their own community." A hum of ayes hung on the air. "You will call to remembrance that I vowed when you elected me, ladies and gentlemen, to always side with our community in a conflict of this sort. Have you any comment, Mr. Parsons?"

"No comment."

"Our entire school board voted to make an exception to the county ruling to allow Mrs. Gibson to take her child, who is well-mannered and well-behaved, into the classroom with her. She has done this with our knowledge and our approval." A nodding of heads assured the mayor of the audience's support. "Has there been any complaint, Mrs. Parsons, that the child acted in a disruptive manner or distracted the classroom in any way?"

"None, sir."

"We feel that the Gap has never had a more qualified teacher who carried the best interests of her pupils in the fiber of her soul. As I told the board at the onset, this woman can teach better with one hand holding to the child's than most teachers can teach with two free hands."

More ayes filled the room. It could not be denied that Mayor Wells was a convincing speaker. He had the sanction of the majority, and he knew it. Voting time would come around again, and they would remember this night.

"Furthermore," he continued, "we all know why Mrs. Gibson chose to keep the child by her side. We know how she lost her husband more than a year ago in an industrial accident at our own quarries, and since that time, her life has been bound up in the child's . . ."

Nathan moved to the edge of his chair as if to assure himself that what he heard was correct. No one had ever informed him that Mrs. Gibson was a widow. When he borrowed the wheel . . . left the note . . . made an effort to buy her property . . . there had been no hint that she was single.

"Your Honor . . ." The voice belonged to Nathan; his sense of propriety made him speak.

"Yes, sir."

"I humbly regret the problems my position as county employee has caused your community. Conscientiously, I could not have done otherwise. I am responsible to see that the rules handed down to me are carried out. That is my job. But since it has come down to my job or the teacher's, I ask that Mrs. Gibson be reinstated immediately. I will be the one to resign my position."

A cheer went up from the crowd, followed by applause. The city had won. Mayor Wells had not expected it to be so easy. Nathan's attitude made criticism impossible. The editor of the town's periodical, pen ready to write an account of the white-hot battle, put away his pad reluctantly.

Dessie found herself on her feet. "Your Honor . . ."

"Yes, Mrs. Gibson?"

"If the decision lies between my job and Mr. Parsons's," she protested, "I will not return to the school to teach. Mr. Parsons is a good man, acting out his principles, and I will not teach unless he remains on as superintendent."

The mayor looked at Dessie helplessly, beseeching-ly. She had messed up his well-laid plan; he had not an-ticipated her move.

"You will not reconsider, Mrs. Gibson?"

She hesitated, looking about the room slowly. All eyes fastened upon her expectantly. Arthur had said she was a key. Was she turning the lock as God would want her to? Nathan's head went down, a suspenseful silence filled the room, and the mayor waited.

"No, sir."

Arthur smiled at her over the crowd. Knowing he was proud of her decision made her feel better.

The meeting might have ended there in a yet unre-solved stalemate had not Mr. Boles moved in from the sidelines, swaggering importantly. "Mr. Mayor . . ."

"Yes, Mr. Boles?" The mayor was tired of Mr. Boles' attention-getting tactics and his voice reflected his irritation.

"Upon my understanding that Mr. Dave Parsons would be here tonight, I have come with legal charges against him."

"You have legal charges against the county superin-tendent?"

"I have, Your Honor."

"Please state your case, Mr. Boles."

"This man brought the teacher's child to me some weeks back. Why he had the child, I do not know. But I do know that he was intoxicated at the time."

"And why have you waited until tonight to press charges, Mr. Boles?"

"I haven't been able to locate the man in question."

"Do you care to respond, Mr. Parsons?"

"I plead not guilty to the charge of drunkenness."

"But you do admit to being in possession of the child?"

"I do, Your Honor."

The newspaper man picked up his pen to write, anticipating a sizzling scoop after all.

"Mrs. Gibson, were you aware of this accusation?"

"No, sir." A case of mistaken identity, no doubt. Nathan Parsons had never "been in possession" of her child, although her child had tried to possess him a couple of times!

The newspaper reporter wrote fast.

"Would you care then to sign the complaint?"

"No, sir," Dessie replied. "I would trust my child to Mr. Parsons's care anytime, anywhere." The words from her heart shocked her ears.

"Have you known this gentleman for a long while, Mrs. Gibson? Is he an acquaintance of your family?"

"I've known him for . . . a very long time." Why had she defended him? Arthur said the man wasn't "good for Becky."

The night-beat officer showed unrestrained disappointment. His hopes for recognition were bashed. The reporter folded his paper.

"Can you prove, Mr. Boles, that Mr. Parsons was drunk? Have you any witnesses?"

"I . . .er, no . . . but . . ."

"Then the case is dismissed," the mayor barked. A bit of a personality clash existed between the mayor and the night patrolman, and the mayor relished exercising his authority over the pushy peace officer. Mr. Boles left the kangaroo court a defeated man, his aspirations of winning the next election over the mayor nothing but ashes.

Nathan's eyes met Dessie's and held. A thrill ran down her spine, sending weakness to her knees and strength to her heart.

Chapter Twenty-Five

Straightening Out the Facts

"*We* received a letter from Mama today," Dessie told Arthur when he came home from work. The letters, always welcomed, now became treasures in a field of days.

Both Dessie and Becky sorely missed the classroom with its babble of learning children. Becky could not understand why they had been barred from the classes; she missed the laughter and companionship that the recesses brought. An emptiness, much like the loss Dessie felt when Walt left her, came back to torment Dessie. She masked her desolation as best she could from her brother, who worked hard to make her happy. Yet she knew that he surmised her inner turmoil.

"What did Mama have to say?" he asked.

"They're having a family reunion at Brazos Point on Thanksgiving. Joseph and Amy and their children are coming from the territory on the Pullman. Chester's coming in from finishing school. All the family will be together but us. They want us to come, too. But of course we can't go."

"Who says we can't?"

"You're a working man, Arthur. Supporting a family."

"I can take off a few days. I work for my men and they work for me."

"It's a bad time of year for traveling, too. We could get weathered in . . . or out."

"Bad weather would hit here before it would there. That's farther south by several miles. If the weather shuts us in at Brazos Point, we can be reasonably sure that I couldn't work here either."

Dessie began packing and planning, filling the vacuous hours with gift-making for each of the family "back home." Time again took wings.

"I'm not sure but that I should have returned with Mama and Papa last summer," she confided to Arthur when at last they started for the community of their nativity. "I could have saved myself and the whole community a lot of inconvenience. My decision to stay in the Gap was based on a crazy dream I had that probably meant nothing at all. The dream ended in a rainbow, and I've seen nothing to indicate a rainbow since then!"

"But just think, Dessie. If you had not stayed in the Gap, I might never have met Lucy!" Arthur gave a coltish laugh.

"What with taking care of me and Becky, I'm afraid you haven't enough time or money for Lucy anyhow."

"Lucy is willing to wait."

Dessie sighed. "It's not fair to make her wait . . . endlessly. I've got to find a way to support myself, Arthur, and not depend on you. But it'll be three more years before Becky is old enough to start to school."

"Three years isn't so terribly long. Jacob waited fourteen for Rachel."

"I guess three years isn't so long when you've . . . hope."

"Will you . . . do you ever plan to remarry, Dessie? If the right one comes along, I mean?"

"I'm not sure, Arthur. It would have to be a special man . . . for me *and* Becky."

"You have never met anyone that could . . . fill your order?"

"I . . . guess not."

"What about Dave? Have you never considered him at all?" The words splashed over the dam of Arthur's resolve to mention neither superintendent nor ex-teacher to the other.

"You're the one that warned me about him."

"Warned you?"

"Yes, you said a man was coming to my house that was 'no-account,' running from his past, and after my property . . ."

"But that man came during the deluge while you were at school, Dessie. I figured it would be best not to worry you by telling you he'd been there."

"Who came?"

"The man from the quarry that I warned you about. Named Slats. He's mended his ways now, though, and sent for his wife and two children. He's making a real family man of himself. I'm almost sorry for the things I said about him."

Dessie's thoughts swam in a whirlpool of perplexity. "You mean, Nath . . . Dave Parsons wasn't the man you indicated wasn't good for me . . . or Becky? You said if

165

any man came not to fall for his line because he'd be lying. And Dave Parsons came to look at my *property*. I spent my time hedging his marriage proposal!"

"Dessie! You mean you thought . . . ?" Arthur threw back his forehead, pounding it with the heel of his hand. "I can't believe you thought I meant *Dave.*"

"It was hard to accept, but you said 'trust me' and I was trying!" defended Dessie, wanting to laugh and cry simultaneously.

"Oh, Dessie, I'm sorry! I wasn't talking about Dave at all! I've never met a more honest man on earth than Dave. I . . . wouldn't have kept company with him had he been a rotter!"

"Do you remember when we were talking about the boardinghouse and I asked if . . . Dave's family lived with him?"

"I remember."

"You said he had no family . . . now. Which indicated that he had had a family at one time. I . . . connected your statement with the one about the married man trying to hide his past."

"The mistake was mine, sis."

"Then what happened to Na . . . Dave's family?"

"Death. He lost a wife and a year-old baby girl within weeks of each other. It left him kind of . . . bitter."

"That's the reason for that . . . look in his eyes when he saw Becky in the classroom the first time he came. It brought back old hurts he was trying to forget."

"You're right."

"But the . . . deep hurt isn't there anymore."

"I noticed that. Since Dave's illness, he's lost most of his bitterness. The loneliness is still there, though."

166

"How long ago has this been, Arthur?"

"Six years."

"And he still . . . hurts?"

"He's had nothing or no one to heal the hurt."

"What brought him to the Gap?"

"He was running from himself. From memories. He thought he could lose himself in his job. But it didn't work."

He even tried changing his name, Dessie said to herself, *but that didn't help.* Then aloud, "Why does he want to buy . . . my house?"

"He's tired of the boardinghouse. The proprietor is bossy and the food lousy. It's a depressing place, really."

"Won't he be more lonely in a house all alone?"

"Yes. He's dreading the winter something fierce. He says he misses his little girl worse than he ever has. Winters are . . . bleak."

"I'm . . . thinking about selling him my house, Arthur . . . if that would make him happy. Since you've told me what you have, I want more than anything for Dave Parsons to be happy again. I . . . know what he's going through."

"Buying a house won't make Dave happy, Dessie. There's only one thing that will bring him happiness again."

"What's that?"

"A wife and a little girl."

Chapter Twenty-Six

Home for Thanksgiving

"*W*ell, what's going on in the territory, Joseph?" Arthur asked, passing his plate to Sally for another helping of apple cobbler.

If Martha noticed that Dessie was distracted she made no mention of it, or else she laid it to lingering grief. Dessie's thoughts kept drifting back to the Gap . . . and to Nathan. Out the window she could see the barn where she had written his name along with her own. *Dessie claims Nathan forever.* The rain had washed it off, but with teen-age determination she had written it back even bigger the second time.

"We got the new school built from Effie's inheritance," Joseph was saying. "It was her dream."

"You remember my brother Jonathan don't you, Dessie?" Amy asked.

Dessie brought her wandering mind into focus. "Yes. He married Sandra Grimes. I went to school with her."

"Sandra teaches in Effie's school during the week, and Jonathan uses the same building on Sundays for church services. He reminds me so much of Matthew. Preaches just like him!"

"We need more hellfire-and-brimstone preachers with th' backbone o' a sawlog." Henry shook his graying head. "Ever'thing's goin' modern an' mostly to th' devil these days."

"I'm sure there's good and bad in all eras, Papa," Matthew noted. "It's up to us to choose the good and shun the evil."

"Sarah got 'er one o' those talkin' machines. They're takin' th' country," fumed Henry. "Imagine sittin' in one house an' talkin' to someone a mile away without leavin' yore chair!"

"It'd be mighty handy in bad weather," Martha commented.

" 'Tain't good fer nuthin' but a gossip line," warned Henry. "Puts women talkin' when they should be listenin'—er workin'. Won't be nary one o' those sinful machines in my house!"

"Th' beaten'st thang is th' horseless carriage." Martha quickly diverted Henry's attention, knowing his aversion for the telephone.

"Yep. First 'twas th' Stanley Steamer. Now, it's these sprocket-driven buggies. What'll they thank up next?"

"An' I hear they might nigh scare th' poor horses outta ten years' growth with their awful noise an' clatter," Martha added.

"I was thinking about getting me one before I lost my teaching job," Dessie admitted sheepishly.

"Dessie!" Martha's mouth flew open. "An' you a lady! Well, I'm right glad you lost yore job if'n you was gonna turn out a flapper."

"Oh, I'd let Arthur drive it," Dessie said quickly to mollify Martha. "I'd be afraid to cross the wooden bridge!"

"Speakin' o' th' bridge, tell us 'bout th' flood o' th' dry gulch," Martha reminded. "You said in yer letter you'd tell it when you seen us next. We're hankerin' fer to hear."

"I was safe and sound at the school when the bridge fell. Arthur and Becky faced the danger."

"I can't tell you a whole lot myself," spoke up Arthur. "When the bridge crumbled, a timber knocked me out cold as a corpse. I came to at the mayor's house with the prettiest little nurse you ever saw!" He winked at Dessie.

Martha gave him a reproachful look for mentioning the nurse. "What happened to our Becky?"

"She must have been thrown into the river. When I came to my senses the next day and found that she was missing, I almost lost my wits again! Here Dessie was across the river not knowing that either of us was in any peril . . . and I couldn't even remember the details of the accident."

"Well, what happened next?" goaded Martha.

"Me and the pretty nurse started praying."

"Then?"

"About that time the night watchman came to the mayor's front door with Becky. We suppose that a passerby—a stranger—pulled her from the boiling waters, but it had been hours since the bridge collapsed when she was brought to us safe. Where she was all that time, we may never know."

"You don't have no idee who fetched 'er out?"

"None."

Becky, being entertained by Joseph's older children, raised her head when she heard her name. *"Nathan* got me out of the water!" she declared emphatically. "I told you. We stayed on a little shelf in the river all night. He covered me with his coat so I wouldn't freeze."

"Nathan?" Dessie's heart gave a mad lurch.

"Yes, Dessie, Becky told me when the watchman brought her to the mayor's that a man named Nathan saved her. I don't know where she picked up that name. There's nobody we know by the name of Nathan."

Dessie stared past them all, deep in thoughts of her own. Fragmented answers to the riddle began to fit into place. "Arthur!" she tried to keep her voice calm. "Didn't you tell me that Dave Parsons was on the bridge with you when it fell?"

"Yes."

"Was he thrown into the river, too?"

"I suppose he was. He didn't say. But he got wet enough to take his death of pneumonia, so he must have been."

The isolated conversation made little sense to the listeners, but Dessie pressed on, feeling she verged on a momentous discovery.

"Do you think . . . could he have *jumped in* to save Becky?"

"I . . . guess he could've. But Becky says the fellow's name was *Nathan.*"

"But remember, Arthur, at the city counsel meeting, the night watchman *accused* Na . . . Dave of 'being in possession of' my child."

"You're not coming through clear, Dessie."

172

"He also accused Dave of being drunk. You say Dave was very ill . . ."

"You're trying to say Becky's Nathan may have been Dave instead?"

"Exactly!"

"Let's talk to Becky. She has the memory of an elephant."

They called the child. "Becky, is the Nathan that got you out of the water the same man that came to school?" Dessie prodded.

Becky nodded her head vigorously, the tight curls springing like a wooden yo-yo. "But you wouldn't let me hug him and say thank you." She looked accusingly at her mother with her wide, innocent eyes.

So that's why she ran to embrace Nathan! He had saved her life! "It was the school superintendent that rescued her, Arthur!" Dessie said triumphantly.

"His name is Nathan." Becky was adamant.

"What makes you think that is his name, Becky?" asked Arthur.

"He told me his name!"

"It seems that it don't make a whole gob o' diff'rence who saved 'er, er what 'is name was, jest so's she was got out alive," pointed out Martha, missing the significance of the discussion.

"Oh, but it does, Mama." Dessie's eyes shone. "The man that saved her life almost lost his own in the effort."

"Well, who was he? An acquaintance o' yorn?"

"He was the county school superintendent—the man that just fired me."

"What a mixup!"

"And now he wants to buy my property in the Gap."

"That's good news, Dessie. I been aprayin' you'd get a buyer. Why don't you sell it t' 'im an' move back here an' teach." Martha latched onto the opportunity to try to persuade Dessie back into her perimetrical shelter. "Now's you've lost yer job there, 'twould be th' proper thang fer you to do."

"I'm considering selling him my place, Mama. He likes it, and it will put him closer to his work. I think he'd be happy there, and I want him to be happy."

"That's a mighty Christian spirit after 'im firin' you an' all, Dessie," boasted Henry. "But then you always was big-hearted."

"He didn't fire me by choice, Papa. He had to stick by his principles, and I admire him for that. And remember . . . he saved your granddaughter's life."

"Then you'll be movin' back soon, Dessie?" A note of triumph sprang up in Martha's voice.

"I . . . I'm not sure . . . what I'll do just yet. There are some things I need to pray about . . ."

Arthur grinned, raising one eyebrow. *Do I know her plans?*

Chapter Twenty-Seven

A Futile Visit

"*W*here are you going, young man?" Mrs. Birmingham peered at Nathan above her horn-rim glasses. "It's turning cold out there."

She means well, he kept repeating to himself to save his sanity, but her nagging made him grit his teeth.

"Uh . . . I'm going to call on a friend."

"The friend can wait. Is the call absolutely necessary?"

"Yes'm."

"If you don't take care of yourself, you'll be back abed."

Nathan pulled the choker about his neck and dashed out the front door, closing it too harshly, forgetting its nondescript lead glass design in his desperation to escape further protests from the aging lady.

The cold slapped at his face, making his eyes smart. The winter that he dreaded lurked just around the corner.

I'll go see her today, he had promised himself when he awoke after dreaming of Dessie's beautiful eyes for two consecutive nights. In the dream she tried to tell him something, but he was never quite close enough to hear what she had to say.

He had questions that begged answering. Mrs. Gibson had said under cross-examination at the council meeting that she had known him for "a very long time." Six months was not a long time. And at the school she had called him Nathan. No one in the area knew his first name unless the child had revealed it.

He had intended to ask his friend, Arthur Harris, if he knew where the teacher hailed from. But Arthur failed to show up in town Saturday; that was unusual. Arthur had been evasive as to where he roomed, and now Nathan wished he had pressed the issue, because if Arthur fell sick, he wouldn't know where to locate him to repay his kindnesses.

Nathan urged his horse to a faster gait and breathed in the damp prewinter air. With his mind made up, nothing but death could keep him from the lady who had defended him, given up her teaching position that he might keep his employment, and kept him from landing in jail on false charges pressed by the night watchman.

Dessie's house came into view after what seemed to Nathan an infinite length of time. No smoke tailed from the chimney to the sky, and the curtains were drawn over closed windows.

The wagon wheel still rested against the house exactly where he had left it. He had assumed by something she said that she was married. But the mayor made it clear that she had been widowed for more than a year now. Dare he hope that she left the wheel where he placed it on purpose? As a reminder of he himself? His humility would not allow the thought to dwell.

He alighted and went to the door, his heart pounding heavily. The door knocker clanged a hollow echo, but no sounds came from within. He lifted the knocker again, knowing it was useless. The place was obviously shut up.

A wave of fright bordering on hysteria commandeered his whole being. *She had sold out and left!* With the loss of her teaching job, that would be the instinctive thing for a widow to do. But she had said she would "let him know" when she was ready to sell.

Perhaps Mr. Davis would know if anyone had bought the place. Nathan remounted the horse and headed toward town.

"If the house is sold, I didn't take care of the transaction," Mr. Davis offered. "Her brother came in and took it off the market list before he left town last week. He said they had found a buyer if she ever decided to sell."

She had had company then. Perhaps she had moved home with her brother and he was handling her business affairs. He had waited too late to call on her! Perhaps he had lost track of her forever. And now he would never know where she had met him or how she knew his name.

Another thought crossed his searching mind. The mayor might know where she had gone. Back out to the mayor's house he sped.

Lucy answered the door. Yes, she said, she could tell him where the teacher had gone. She had returned to her home community.

Nathan requested the address. The name Brazos Point struck a familiar note in his memory, but the name Gibson remained tantalizingly vague. If he just knew her maiden name . . .

A fog shrouded the countryside so heavily that the cloud-like density made traveling back to the boarding-house slow and laborious. Mrs. Birmingham stood at the door awaiting his return. He dared not tell her that his throat ached and his chest burned like fire. His greatest ambition was to squeeze past her to the solitude of his room and write a letter.

Dear Mrs. Gibson:

I called at your house today, but you were not at home. I obtained your whereabouts from Miss Lucy Wells and have presumed upon your goodness that you will accept a few words from my pen.

I failed to avail myself of the opportunity to thank you for defending me at the council meeting. I wouldn't have minded forfeiting my job, but to be disgraced with a record of public drunkenness against my name would have brought me much grief of mind.

The meeting raised many questions in my mind. You testified that you had known me for a great length of time, and at the school you called me by the name my mother chose to call me at birth. Have we met before?

I apologize for my ignorance of your widowhood. I can certainly sympathize with your feelings. Please pardon any brusqueness on my part that could have caused you pain.

I trust that you plan to return to the Gap and request the pleasure of calling on you there.

May I hear from you?

Yours truly,
Nathan David Parsons

By the time the letter reached its destination, Dessie and Arthur were on their way back to the Gap. Martha fussed that they cut their visit short, but Dessie handled her well.

"I need to get back and make some plans for my future, Mama," she had said. Martha interpreted the statement to fit her own fancy: Dessie was rushing home to pack and return.

"Dessie got a letter," Martha told Henry. "Shall we post it on to 'er?"

"Looks like it jest come from where she's headed, Martha."

"Wonder who 'tis from?"

"Who does th' back say?"

"N. Parsons."

"Why, Martha, I do believe that's th' name o' that evangelist's son that played th' geetar what she was so sweet on when she was a sixteen-year-old lassie!"

"Th' one she writ 'is name on th' barn?"

"That 'un."

"Wonder how he happened to find 'er after all these years?"

"I dunno, Martha. I reckon fate decides some things."

Chapter Twenty-Eight

Nathan's Resignation

"*W*e scarcely get home and you hie yourself off!" scolded Dessie playfully, watching Arthur adjust his collar stays. He had brought his "courting clothes" back with him from Brazos Point.

"Mrs. Wells said Lucy was in town . . ."

"If she's there, you'll find her!"

"And buy her a soda. And I thought I might run across my old friend, Dave Parsons."

Dessie followed him to the short front stoop. "Give Mr. Parsons my regards." Her voice rang with light-hearted carelessness. "It's time my wheel of fortune starts spinning." She pointed toward the wagon wheel against the house.

"Yes, because if it doesn't go to work pretty soon, I'm going to cart it off to the shed!" laughed Arthur.

Dessie dusted the furniture, baked a custard pie, and read a Bible story to Becky while Arthur was gone. Anything to pass the time!

She eagerly anticipated his return with news from

Nathan, but when he walked in the door, she knew something was wrong.

"Didn't you find Lucy, Arthur?" she asked anxiously.

"I found her okay."

"Has she found herself another beau in your absence?"

"Nope. I bought her a soda."

"What about Mr. Parsons?"

"Mr. Parsons wasn't there."

"Out on one of his routes probably."

"No." Arthur avoided her eyes. "Apparently he moved away while we were gone."

"Na . . . *Dave* moved away?"

"Lucy said he turned in his resignation as county school superintendent. Mailed it to the mayor. Last week. Hasn't been seen since."

Dessie's bubble of happiness burst, shattering into a million pieces, leaving nothing but an empty desolation.

"You . . . have no idea where he went?"

"No, I don't. I think he was from somewhere in Louisiana."

"I guess the poor man couldn't bear the winter here . . . alone."

"You can probably have your old teaching job back now, Dessie."

"I don't want the job back now."

"You don't?"

"No. Teaching was just a transition to get me past the worst of my . . . sense of loss. What I want is a complete family again."

"I'll . . . sure miss Dave."

"Is there anyway we . . . you can trace him—through

182

the boardinghouse perhaps?"

"That's an idea. I can try. Mrs. Birmingham will know where he went if anyone does."

"I need his address . . . to thank him for saving Becky. I am indebted to him."

Arthur called at Mrs. Birmingham's rooming house the following Saturday. When he asked for Dave, she sighed wearily. "He's back down again," she complained. "I caught him sneaking in a few nights ago when the fog was so thick you could cut it with a knife. I'd warned him about leaving, but he wouldn't listen. Now I'm afraid he's in serious trouble."

"May I see him?" Arthur planned to see his friend, Dave, regardless of the proprietor's objections.

"I shouldn't let anyone in to see him. He needs rest, but . . ."

"He wants to talk with me about something." A statement of faith.

Something like holy hush filled Nathan's room. He had been praying. "Pull up a chair, Arthur," he said. "Where have you been keeping yourself?"

"I made a little Thanksgiving trip to visit relatives."

"That's what Lucy said."

"And Lucy tells me that you may be leaving us."

Nathan gave an empty laugh that brought on a nasty fit of coughing. "I'll have to get better before I can go anywhere!"

"You must take better care of yourself, Dave."

"I . . . needed to make a call. Tell me, Arthur, do you know where the teacher, Mrs. Gibson, moved?" His tone was urgent.

"She didn't move."

"Mr. Davis told me that her brother came and took over her affairs and that he had a buyer for the property. The house was all closed up, so I assumed that she returned with him to his home."

He's talking about me! Arthur surpressed his mirth. "She's back now. I saw a light in the window . . . last night."

"Do you know—have you heard—if she plans to move . . . soon?"

"I don't think so."

"I . . . didn't realize she was widowed until the night of the council meeting. I've . . . resigned my job, Arthur. Now perhaps she can get her old job back. Of course, that's not the reason I resigned. I wouldn't want her to think that."

"She won't take the job back."

"How do you know?"

"She told me she wouldn't."

"How will she survive . . . financially?"

"Her brother supports her."

"I see. He must be quite wealthy. Do you happen to know where she's from originally?"

"She's from a little place in central Texas called Brazos Point. Hardly big enough to be listed on the map."

"I've been there."

Arthur showed mild surprise. "You've been to Brazos Point?"

"Years ago. With my father. I don't think I've ever told you, but my father was a traveling preacher. I went with him a lot in my younger years. If my memory serves me right, the community was just a bunch of farmers with a school and a clapboard church . . ."

"Your memory serves you right."

"They put up a brush arbor, and we were to conduct a protracted meeting there. But we had scarcely got started when word came that my mother was desperately ill. She died shortly thereafter, and we never returned to finish the revival."

Mental pictures of his home town, drawn by Nathan, made Arthur smile. He changed the subject lest he give himself away. "What do you plan to do now that you have given up your school job?"

"Keep my promise to God."

Chapter Twenty-Nine

God's Mysterious Ways

"*I* felt the call of God on my life to preach when I was quite young, fourteen or fifteen. I promised God that I would dedicate my life to the spreading of His gospel. But I . . . felt I couldn't. I renewed that vow when death came to claim me this fall." Nathan told his story slowly, deliberately, making no excuses for his failures.

Arthur listened as the contents of Nathan's heart spilled out.

"I tried to run from God and forget the vow."

"Would it be all that hard to be a preacher?"

"For most people it wouldn't. But for me, it was. On account of my father, whom I love dearly."

"I . . . don't understand."

"It's a long story, and I don't want to bore you."

"I assure you I won't be bored." Arthur pulled his chair closer to the bedside. "There's nothing to keep me from listening all day . . . and all night if necessary."

Nathan smiled feebly. "It won't take that long." He resituated his pillow and took a sip of water from the pewter pitcher on the tea cart. "I had studied the Bible for days, finding many passages that I could not understand. It seemed a very conflicting book. When I went to my father, his explanations were always vague. 'There's no way to *understand* the Godhead,' he said, 'just believe and accept it.'

"I tried, plagued with unanswered questions. But I'm just not the 'believe and accept it' kind, if it doesn't correspond with the Bible. Then, in my late teens I met a young man that I'll never forget if I live to be a hundred. He was a preacher, too, with the most beautiful wife I'd ever laid eyes on. She had blue, blue eyes and golden-colored hair. His name was Matthew, and her name was Pauline. Over the years, I've forgotten the last name."

He's talking about my own brother. Arthur swallowed hard.

"This young preacher had discovered a doctrine in the Bible that he called the mighty God in Jesus Christ. I had never heard anything quite like it, but when I heard it, I knew that I had come face to face with truth and would never be able to preach my father's trinity doctrine again.

"When I approached my father with it, he reacted violently, saying it was heresy. I was shocked, thinking that if it was in the Bible in black and white, he would accept it."

"This doctrine—what was it?" asked Arthur.

"Father's doctrine called for three persons in the Godhead instead of simply one God as the Bible teaches. I could never quite comprehend how the Holy Ghost was a *person*. The Holy Ghost is a Spirit—the Holy *Spirit!* God's Spirit fell on the believers on the Day of Pentecost.

The Holy Spirit is the Spirit of Christ; Jesus will dwell within us in Spirit form if we let Him. Jesus said He would go away and send His Spirit back to dwell in us. It wasn't a *person* He sent back.

"And *God* is a Spirit. The Bible says so. Why, He's everywhere! He isn't confined to a human body. So that leaves only one person of the Godhead—the human person Jesus Christ. 'To wit, that God was in Christ, reconciling the world unto himself.' That's in II Corinthians five and nineteen. Jesus is 'the image of the invisible God;' Colossians one and fifteen tells us. As a man Jesus was the *only begotten* Son of God; the Spirit of God was made manifest through Him.

"The whole Bible from Genesis to Revelation fell into place before my very eyes. I had never been so happy— or enlightened. I had found truth. Father kept saying, 'God the Father, God the Son, and God the Holy Ghost.' I tried to explain to him that the *Holy Ghost* overshadowed Mary and she conceived, making the Holy Ghost and the Father synonymous.

" 'John had this marvelous revelation,' I told Father. 'In the very first verse of his book he said the Word was God and in the fourteenth verse he said the Word became flesh and dwelt among us, speaking of Jesus.' But Father fought the new light with everything in him.

"Matthew said he baptized differently, too. Since all the fulness of the Godhead dwells in Jesus bodily according to Colossians two and nine, and since Jesus is the only name given among men whereby we must be saved according to Acts four twelve, he baptizes in the name of Jesus. Jesus told us in Matthew, chapter twenty-eight and verse nineteen, to be baptized in the *name* of the Father,

Son and Holy Ghost. Father isn't a name; neither is Son or Holy Ghost. The *name* that reveals the Godhead is Jesus!

"Well, Arthur, I got my Bible down and started searching. Everybody that was baptized into the New Testament church was baptized in the name of Jesus. I was amazed!

"I had no problem understanding about being filled with the Holy Spirit. I received the Holy Spirit before I . . . lost my wife and baby. She didn't believe like I did, so I kept my beliefs pretty well to myself."

Nathan lapsed into a peaceful calm of meditation, closing his eyes. "I'm . . .Mrs. Birmingham thinks I'm in for a bad spell like I had before . . . but I'm not. I have too much work to do for God. I quit the school job to . . . preach."

"Where?"

"God hasn't let me know yet."

"Dave, I have something to tell you."

"Say on. I can take it. Nothing or nobody can . . . pull me from the truth now. I've . . . renewed my vow to God."

"I believe every word you've said. Matthew is my brother."

"Matthew . . . Harris! That was the name! Why didn't I . . . ? Nathan chuckled. "And he's your brother? Well, doesn't God work in mysterious ways!"

"I just saw him last week. In fact, he'll be coming out to see me and . . . er, soon."

"Good! I'll be well enough for him to baptize me when he comes. My appetite is coming back. Will you see if Mrs. Birmingham happens to have some potato soup left from lunch?"

Arthur left and came back with a bowl of hot soup.

"And one more question, Arthur."

"Yes, sir."

"Do you know if Mrs. Gibson is a Christian or not?"

"Yes, she is. She believes the Bible just like you do."

Chapter Thirty

Dessie's Rainbow

Let Mrs. Birmingham fuss.

The sun shown warmly on the winter fields as Nathan made his way, drawn by the magnet of his heart, to Dessie's house. Had he but known her circumstances when he borrowed the wagon wheel . . .

She answered his knock, but her face registered no surprise—only joy—at the sight of the tall, statuesque man on the short front stoop. His shadow, falling on dried grass, was but a short one now; summer's long shadows had ended.

Becky smiled up at him with sparkling eyes but made no move from her station behind her mother's skirt. "Hi, Nathan!" she chirped.

He returned her smile. "May I come in, Mrs. Gibson?"

The silvery winter sun sent streams of light splashing across the jade-green dress, the color reflecting into her soft eyes. A girlish rush of excitement, buried ten years ago, resurrected and painted her cheeks.

He took a chair, and she brought him a cup of hot coffee. "Arthur said you had been ill," she mentioned.

"Yes, but I'm on the mend. I . . . came to offer my apologies."

"Apologies for what? For standing for right?" Dessie's voice was soft.

"No. For being county school superintendent in the first place."

"You were a good one."

"But that wasn't God's will for my life. Because I was out of pocket with Him, I messed up your career, too."

"I . . . I'm not interested in a career. I just took the position to fill the . . . loneliness."

"I . . . understand. Did you get my letter?"

"Your letter? What letter, sir?"

"I wrote to you at Brazos Point."

"No, I didn't get it. I . . . guess we had already started back before it was delivered."

"I . . . wrote to thank you for defending me at the council meeting."

"I didn't want you to lose your job."

"I wouldn't have minded losing my job. It's the record of public drunkenness that I couldn't bear."

"I know . . . you wouldn't drink."

"Thank you for your confidence in me."

"And I want to thank you for saving Becky's life. I . . . just recently found out it was you."

"I'm not sure but that she saved my life. Her courage astounded me. I . . . without her brave trust, I might have given up. How . . . did you find out?"

"You must have told Becky your real name."

"And she told you?"

"No, I already knew."

194

The mahogany eyes searched her face. "How did you . . . know my name?"

"I . . . wrote it on the barn when I was sixteen years old."

Nathan grappled for comprehension. "Why did you . . . write my name on your barn?"

"I had a crush on the handsome guitar player that came to a brush arbor meeting with his father. So I wrote on the barn, 'Dessie claims Nathan forever.' The rain washed it off, but I wrote it again."

"Dessie! Not Dessie Harris?"

"Dessie Harris . . . Gibson."

"You . . . knew who I was all the time?"

"Yes, I recognized you when you came to borrow the wheel."

"Dessie . . . does the claim you wrote on the barn still stand?"

"The rains of life washed it away . . . but I wrote it back when . . . Arthur told me you, too, were a widower."

The dizzy, head-spinning flashback . . . it happened again as Nathan took her hand in his own.

Arthur whistled through the door. He stopped abruptly. "Why, hello, Dave. I see you're feeling better."

"He's Nathan, Arthur," corrected Becky defensively.

"Nathan David Parsons," Nathan grinned. "I've come to tell . . . Dessie that I love her."

"But I do, too!" Arthur objected, in good-humored fun.

Nathan dropped Dessie's hand. "I'm sorry, Arthur. You didn't tell me. I thought you were courting Lucy. I didn't know you . . ."

"I'm Dessie's *brother,* Nathan David Parsons! You

go right on loving her. Nothing would please me more. In this case, we can share!"

"Arthur *Harris!* Of course! You mean you have lived right in this house all the time with my . . . sweetheart, and I didn't know it?"

"You like to have caught me a time or two!" Arthur chortled. "Especially when you came to buy our house!"

"Arthur, I . . . you . . . I ought to . . ."

"You didn't know you were fishing my niece from the river, did you?"

"Come here, darling." Nathan dropped to one knee and beckoned for Becky, taking her into his arms. "Would it be all right if I marry your mommy and be your daddy?"

Becky didn't answer. Instead, a hot tear was transferred from her soft pink cheek to his bronzed leathery one as she nodded her head and clung to him, tightening her arms about his neck.

"I have a confession to make, Arthur," Dessie smiled impishly. "I knew who Nathan was all the time."

"I . . . don't understand."

"I wrote his name on our lopsided barn when I was sixteen. The message said, 'Dessie claims Nathan forever.' Of course, you were too young to pay any attention."

"Dessie! Nathan was your beau . . . your first beau?" He stopped, scratching his head.

"Ten years ago."

"I think the wheel of fate is working, Dessie. I'm glad you insisted on me leaving it in the yard." Arthur winked mischievously.

"And I'm ready to buy your sister's property, Arthur. On one condition."

"What's that?"

"That the lady and little girl go with it."

"Then you plan to stay here, Dave?"

"This town needs a church that preaches . . . the truth like Matthew Harris preaches it. I haven't told you yet, Dessie, but I've made a promise to God. Do you object to being wed to a preacher?"

"No objections!" laughed Dessie, feeling the fireworks that she felt a decade ago. "I already have us some converts, Nathan!"

"I guess we'd best send Matthew a telegram," suggested Arthur. "He needs to get here right away to perform this wedding."

He turned his back toward Dessie, uncontrollable emotions threatening his composure. No one deserved this happiness more than Dessie and "Dave."

The city he had learned to love lay in the distance, visible through the sitting-room window. A perfect rainbow, stretching from sky to earth, formed a bridge from the heavens to the Gap. Dessie's rainbow!

Love is filling the Gap, he rejoiced. First it reached to Slats and Beatrice Cunningham. Then to Nathan and Dessie. Now it could reach him . . .

And Lucy.